ZAR

Book One in the Galaxy Gladiators
Alien Abduction Romance Series

Alana Khan

Temptation of the Horizontal LLP

Copyright

Contents

Trope Alert

The HERO AND HEROINE are ordered to mate.

Slavery, violence. history of abuse.

Chapter One

PRESENT DAY

Somewhere in Space

Anya

Someone is screaming. I must be dreaming because I went to sleep on my comfy mattress, yet I feel like I'm lying on cold, hard metal. What's going on?

My eyes pop open, but my brain isn't fully online yet. Was I drugged? My head feels like it's split wide open. As my eyes focus, I notice other bodies lying on the floor nearby. My heart beats like a jackhammer when I see boots that belong on the feet of some post-apocalyptic Mad Max character.

The pain is too real—I'm not dreaming. I make an end run around my rising panic and order my brain to engage. I glance up past black boots to leather-clad calves and see they are wrapped around the feet and legs of something definitely not human. I may not have had my morning cuppa joe, but my brain is now making lightning-fast synaptic con-nections. It doesn't take a rocket scientist to recognize that the creature resembling a humanoid boar who is currently pointing a gun at my chest is an alien.

Sweat blooms on my upper lip and my eyes widen in fright as I absorb what's going on.

I thought aliens from other planets were the stuff of sci-fi movies and *National Enquirer* abduction stories. This isn't fiction. This is real! I order my brain to comply with whatever they ask and force my hands to stop trembling. Job number one is to stay alive.

Crap, he sees my eyes are open and signals with his gun for me to get up. I may be disoriented, but I'm not crazy enough to argue with the business end of that weapon. I stumble toward a couple of human women forming a line behind another boar-man. This one grunts at me and I can't help but notice these guys have four short tusks protruding up from their bottom jaw. Holy shit... tusks!

I get in line behind two women in their twenties like me. One is in baby doll pajamas, the other is wearing only a pair of black boxers with small red hearts. I'm the one from Colorado in a cute flannel two-piece number with a moose on it. Have we all been kidnapped from Earth in our sleep?

"What's happening here?" the petite redhead in the front of the line asks, earning her a hard thump on the head by the butt of boar-man number two's gun.

Rule number one, no talking. Check. Other women are shakily standing up at the first guy's command. We're forming an impeccably ordered line. I'm obeying every direction, even as icy terror races along my veins.

A third boar enters, fumbling with a handful of tech gear. I realize these are glorified collars as he fastens one around each of our necks, and trust me, he's not gentle about it. Screens on the walls jump to life and a video plays. It does not have high production value, but the message is crystal clear.

We all watch, horror growing, as the video depicts a collar being snapped on a reptilian alien's neck. The picture shifts to a close-up of some alien version of a smart watch on an extremely hairy arm. An equally hairy hand pushes a button on the watch and voilà, cut to the poor victim being shocked at what appears to be a torturous level. His eyes widen and his alien mouth pulls back into a rictus of agony as he screams, a sound so chilling the hair on the back of my neck stands up.

Now there's a shot of the watch being dialed higher, and then a gruesome close-up of the victim screeching in pain, his eyes rolling backward. His knees hit the floor as he claws at his neck, trying to remove the collar. With no additional warning, I hear a loud pop and his head explodes right off his shoulders. My knees sag, but I don't allow myself to sink to the floor. I hear the sound of someone retching a little in the back of her mouth, but I can guarantee no one is uttering a word of protest.

Don't fuck with these guys. Point taken.

My horror escalates, my heart hammering in fear, as we're marched into an adjoining room. One by one, we're given a painful shot behind the right ear. No doubt what this is for because now the alien gibberish isn't gibberish anymore. The translator they implanted allows me to understand the angry orders they are barking.

"You're on the *Warbird One* in deep space. You're now the property of the MarZan cartel. Follow!" the boar at the head of the line commands.

My head reels at this information. It was obvious they kidnapped me from my home on Earth, but to hear myself called property spears a sharp arrow of terror through my body.

I'm being as compliant as possible. I'm no fool. No one's coming to save me, I'm too cynical to believe that. I need to figure a way out of this mess. Even as I attempt to control my rising panic, I struggle to get a mental image of every room, hallway, and door—trying to keep track of the layout of this place.

The floors and walls are metal. Everything is utilitarian with no frills. There's been no attempt to make anything attractive or homey. Stark lights shine brightly from above. I see doors, but I don't know where they might lead. I have no idea the scope of the ship, how many floors, or rooms, or aliens might be lurking down hidden corridors.

I take note of how many of these ugly aliens I see, how heavily armed they are, and who's in charge. If there is a way off this ship and back home to Earth, I need to find it.

Terrified of being punished for looking behind me, I sneak a quick peek at how many of us there are—maybe ten human women walking briskly in this fast-paced line. There are four guards, all muscled, wide, ugly pig-like males covered in medieval-looking brown leather pants and tunics.

In addition to the four short tusks protruding up from their bottom jaws, they have porcine noses, and two small horns on the top of their heads. They each have a baton fastened to one side of their belt and a gun fastened to the other. With a rifle slung over one shoulder and the smart watch torture thingy on one wrist, they look ready for battle.

We're forced into a corridor that looks like it's straight out of a low-budget fifties jailhouse movie. Cell after cell comprised of three impenetrable-looking metal walls and a fourth wall of bars facing the hallway. Each room is about eight feet square, with one small bed, a toilet, and a sink. My mind is only registering this information peripherally because my primary focus is on the inhabitants of the cells.

I glimpse the alien in the first cell. He's pushing seven feet tall with thick, ropey muscles. He looks kind of Neanderthal with a short, slightly flattened forehead, and shaggy hair and beard. His jaw is set and tight, his weight is on the balls of his feet, and his brown eyes look flat and dead.

Two of the boar guys flank both sides of his door. Poised in battle stances, their raised guns tell me they won't allow any pushback from us women—or the gargantuan alien in the cell. On high alert, the boar to the right of the door points his gun at the alien in the enclosure. "Face the back wall! On your knees, hands on your head!" The guy instantly pivots, then sinks to his knees.

The boar-guy at the head of the line pushes the redhead in the pink PJs into the cell as if she weighs little more than a bag of groceries. He slams the door shut behind her and keeps the line moving. I'm worried for the redhead, but I don't dare give her even another passing glance. The guards are antsy and look as if they're itching to use their weapons.

At the door to the second cell, the guards go through the same routine. They throw boxer girl into the cell with a fairly humanoid-looking guy. He's humongous—so muscled he makes Conan the Barbarian look puny. He has a robotic left arm and a prosthetic eyepiece that shines red. He's heavily scarred on his face, right arm, and bare torso. He's the more "human" of the two males I've seen. This realization spikes a shiver up my spine. He looks strong enough to kill with his bare hands. The feral glance he tosses over his shoulder after the bars clang closed shows no compassion for the human female in his cell.

Before we move toward the third cell, the boar at the head of the line asks no one in particular, "How are we going to get her into his cell? He has the highest record of kills in the arena. I doubt he'll get on his knees without a fight."

"Fuck him," another responds. "Shock the shit out of him until he's out cold, then throw her in." He doesn't wait for any argument, just presses his watch and turns up the dial until I hear the alien in the next cell roar in pain so loudly my ears ring. Then I hear a thud, which I assume means his body hit the floor.

"You're next, human," one of them orders me. "Let's see if you're alive tomorrow." His tusky laugh chills the marrow in my bones.

Fearful of what my new cellmate looks like, I'm afraid to step around the boar at the front of the line. But I'm too terrified of the guards to dawdle, so I take one step forward. One of the guards impatiently tosses me on the floor of the cell next to my comatose cellmate.

The seven other human females in line gape in horror at the scene in my cell, then continue forward without missing a step.

The alien I'm imprisoned with is clearly out cold. His cheek pressed to the hard gray floor. Although I have nothing to fear from him at this moment, my guts are churning as if they're in a blender.

This guy is enormous, although it's hard to tell how tall he is because he's in a crumpled heap. He's facing away from me, but it's impossible not to notice his massively wide, furred shoulders, slender waist, muscular thighs, and limp tail. Tail! He's got a tail! He's wearing only a primitive fabric loincloth covering little more than his sex.

I scoot over between him and the back wall so I can see his face. I involuntarily gasp in shock. Although his facial shape is human, the features are feline. His nose is wider and flatter than a human's, and there is a groove slashing from nose to upper lip. His body fur is golden, his mane and the tuft at the tip of his tail are dark mahogany. He has a tiny white dot where each of his short whiskers emerges from around his flattened nose.

Even though he's unconscious, his slightly parted lips reveal canines which are frighteningly long and sharp. His hands and feet are more humanoid than feline, with fingers and toes rather than paws. I see no fingernails under the close-cropped fur, but I wonder if he has some sharp retractable claws hiding under there.

He looks like power and grace, even as he lies on the floor, unmoving. It's obvious he's been through a lot. There are raised, discolored remnants of deep cuts all over, but his back is badly scarred in a pattern that could only come from a whip—many whippings. I don't think this creature's had an easy life.

I'll probably never get another chance to give him such a close inspection, so I reach out with one finger and gently touch his shoulder, wondering what his fur feels like.

As swift as lightning, he opens his eyes and grabs my arm. He lithely sits up on his haunches, squeezes my forearm so hard it takes my breath away, and growls. His grip is like steel. I yelp and try to pull back. His fingers tighten and I immediately decide there is no reason to resist. I'm completely overpowered.

His golden feline eyes bore into mine as he squeezes my arm, and a low growl escapes the back of his throat. I have no idea if he even possesses receptive speech, so I use body language to acquiesce. Gazing at the floor, I slump my shoulders in submission.

"Never. Touch. Me. Again," he snarls.

"Absolutely." I'm still looking downward, making myself as small and non-threatening as possible. He probably out-weighs me by double and is strong enough to throw me twenty feet. I've seen enough jailhouse movies to realize we've just established dominance in this cell and he's definitely in charge.

He flings my arm away as if I have leprosy, gets to his feet in one agile move, stalks to the bed, and sits. Okay, I get it. One bed—it's yours. I'll figure out how to manage on the hard, cold floor. He lays down, taking up the entire width of the bunk, which seems narrower than a twin bed.

I wonder if he's going to sleep, but when I finally work up the courage to glance at him, I see he's still piercing me with a predatory stare. In his culture, staring must not be rude, because he's not even pretending to be sly about it. His animalistic "don't fuck with me" look speaks volumes.

I crab-walk backward until my back is tucked against the corner of the rear wall. It's as safe as I'm going to get. No one can sneak up behind me. I'll be ready for a frontal attack, although I have no idea how I'd protect myself from him. Between his sharp teeth and all those muscles, I might as well kiss my ass goodbye.

He's lying on the bed and seems content with that position for right now. I pull my knees up under my chin and try to figure out what to do. In the span of an hour, I've been kidnapped by aliens, collared, chipped, and thrown into a tiny cell with a lion-man. An angry, feral, alpha lion-man who's still staring me down. At this moment, I can see no escape, no pathway to safety, no way home.

As I inspect where he grabbed my arm to see if I have a bruise, I notice my hands are trembling. I'm blinking rapidly to keep tears from sliding down my cheeks, and my chin is quivering so hard I tuck my head down behind my knees to hide my fear.

I've always been a glass half full kind of girl, so I try hard to find the silver lining—any silver lining. The best I can do is to be thankful that I went to sleep last night wearing more than a pair of boxer shorts.

Zar

Propping my torso against the wall behind the length of the bed, I put my hands behind my head, elbows out, and stare at this new female. I've never seen this species before. She must have adequate intelligence since she was smart enough to back off and has the sense not to challenge me.

It's kind of shocking a species like hers evolved on any planet. She has very little muscle mass, no visible claws or talons, no barbed tail, not even sharp teeth that I can see. Perhaps her planet has no natural predators? She wouldn't last a *minima* in the gladiator ring.

Her face seems bland, with no distinguishing features. Perhaps they make good breeders because I can't see any other attraction.

I'm caught off guard as a pang of concern for her flashes through my mind. I shouldn't care. It's everyone for themselves in my world. But it must be shocking for an unprotected female to wake up aboard a slave ship on its way to a gladiator breeding planet. I wonder if her species has evolved enough to even comprehend space travel. She looks completely petrified.

We both seem startled when an announcement interrupts from overhead speakers.

"You have one *hoara* to breed with your cellmate. If you do not complete the act, we will execute both occupants of the cell."

I sigh heavily, my jaw tensing. I am sick to death of being forced to breed.

Anya

Oh no! Hell no! Just no! Can I please catch a break? They want me to breed? With angry lion-man?

I glance over, expecting him to be sprouting a raging hard-on in his loincloth, ready to pounce. Interesting. He looks even less enthused than I am. His face went slack and his eyes dulled.

The loudspeaker repeats the announcement, this time with more urgency. Clearly, they mean business. My mind is spinning and I'm a jumble of emotions, from disbelief to fear to a hell of a lot of anger at this whole situation. I briefly consider refusing the order, but a picture of that unfortunate alien's head exploding flashes through my mind.

"Take your pants off. Get in bed," he urges softly, sounding more resigned than horny.

I'm still in a tight ball in the corner. Pulling a shaky hand across my forehead, I wipe the beads of cold sweat off my brow. Afraid of what this huge alien will do to my body, I'm paralyzed.

"They'll kill you if you don't follow orders. Get up," his tone sounds urgent and... concerned? I guess so. His head will explode as well as my own if we don't comply.

A guard stalks to the front of our cell and points to the collar controller on his wrist. When I don't immediately leap to my feet, his fingers mimic his head exploding, complete with gruesome sound effects. This propels me out of my paralysis and toward the bed.

There's no reason to balk or argue. We're both invested in making this happen. I'm sure neither one of us wants to earn their punishment. I slip under the thin blanket, then shimmy out of pants and panties and toss them to the floor. My heart is hammering now, not in sexual excitement but in all-out abject fear. Do I remember something about cats back on Earth having barbed penises?

Lion guy has untied his loincloth and, although his cock is flaccid, it looks enormous. Even if his equipment doesn't stab or sting, I'm not sure that's going to fit. Thankfully, it looks pretty human, albeit humongous, and I don't see any barbs.

"Get yourself ready," he announces almost robotically, then takes himself in hand. His powerful right hand strokes his length from base to tip and back. He appears as emotionally engaged as when I'm making tuna salad. He seems to be using a practiced stroke from a time-worn formula to get down to business.

As I watch, I catch his deep, feline frown as he notices I'm not getting busy. Before he can scold me, I cover my face with the blanket, slam my eyes shut, and slip my fingers toward my happy spot. I have a time-worn formula, too. Even with this awful situation, between my efforts and a little spit, I think I'm ready.

I peek out from the covers to see lion guy is steel hard and ready for action.

"I'm... I'm ready," my voice is whisper-soft and shy. I slip back under the covers like a prairie dog hurrying to hide in its den.

"Turn over." This is an order. I do as I'm told and get on all fours. This entire day, this entire process, is so surreal. I'll pretend I'm in a dream. I can't afford to tune in to my panic right now. I just have to go through the motions and get this over with. The picture of that alien's head exploding is a strong incentive to do what I must in this tiny bed.

He slips the covers up, and then I feel his weight on the bed. He gently lifts my middle, fits himself behind me, then dispassionately slips a finger inside me. Satisfied I'm ready, he presses his cock against my entrance and waits, giving me time to adjust. He eases in gently, then pulls back, then presses in slightly more. If I'm not mistaken, he's trying hard to give my body time to accommodate his enormous equipment.

There's nothing sensual here. Neither of us is interested in enjoyment. I have to give him credit; he's trying his best not to hurt me. The way he's managing this process, giving my body time to adapt to this invasion, seems far more considerate than I would have ever expected. When he's finally fully seated inside me, he executes three carefully disciplined thrusts, grunts no louder than a sigh, and completely retreats.

His mouth comes close to my ear, his furred, chest touching my back for the first time. His warm breath fans my cheek as his husky voice whispers, "I'm sorry."

Chapter Two

ANYA

I'm not sure my life could get any weirder. The entire landscape of my existence has turned upside down in the last few hours. I don't have the heart to even think about the goal of this little exercise, which must be to impregnate me with lion-man sperm. I don't want to envision the half human/half lion whose cells might be multiplying in my uterus right this very moment. Despite my efforts, my mind flashes me a picture of an alien baby. A frisson of fear bolts up my spine.

I'm trying desperately not to feel sorry for myself or worry about what the future holds or wonder where I am or where they're taking me. Forbidding myself to think of Mom, Dad, my two sisters, and my great friends back in Denver, I give myself permission to mourn their loss later. I need to focus on this moment. Right now I need to pee, clean my leaky nether regions, and get back to the corner of my cell to take just a few minutes to cry. I think I've earned it.

After the peeing and cleaning, but before my well-earned complete nervous breakdown, I hear a commotion coming from down the hall. The solid walls between cells only allow me to see the metal wall through the front bars of my cell. It sounds like the guards are taking the girls out, then returning them. Whatever is going on out there, and however awful it is to be in this cell, fear flares, clenching in my belly.

Lion guy is lounging on the bed, leaning against the wall again. I can tell by his blank expression that he's checked out. I'm glad he wasn't watching me on the toilet. I think I've had all the mortification I can stand.

"What's your name?" If I don't distract myself, I'm going to completely lose my mind. Besides, I'm tired of thinking of him as Lion Guy.

"Zar."

"I'm Anya, thanks for asking," I snap, then pause, wondering if more venom is going to spew out. I'm hovering between two emotions. Part of me is on the cusp of unleashing a blistering tirade at him, blaming him for the fact his sperm is trailing down my thigh at this very moment. But I know he was no more a willing participant in what just happened than I was. The other part of me just wants to collapse in a heap on the floor and go completely catatonic.

"This is the worst day of my life." I'm proud that didn't come across as a moan or an accusation. It sounded factual, because it's the truth.

I'm standing across from him, hands fisted to keep control of my emotions, which are toggling from abject fear to roiling anger. My teeth are clenched, and every muscle in my body is tightly coiled.

I'm about to launch into an angry monologue, then stop abruptly, like the wind unfurled from my sails. It's not his fault. He didn't ask for this any more than I did. Look at him. He's in his own little world, no happier than I am. My emotional rollercoaster speeds right past anger and stops at sadness.

"Don't cry, Anya," I whisper to myself even as hot liquid gathers behind my eyes and my chin quivers. "Shit." I don't want to cry. Crying feels like weakness, but I can't control the tears now snaking down my cheeks.

He shakes his head, bringing himself back to the present, then gives me full eye contact for the first time since we met. He stares for a long moment, then leans toward me, elbows on his thighs.

"There's no way to make this easy for you." His eyes search the ceiling as he appears to fish for something to say. "Being a slave is a hard life. It's unpleasant to know you have no choices, no control over even your own body, that you must do everything the guards order. I'm sorry you had to endure..." His gaze flicks to the bed.

"I hate to be the one to tell you that your old life, whatever it was, will never return." He looks at me directly and adds gently, "There is no escape."

Two tusk guys appear at the cell door as if on cue. Zar is already on his knees, facing the back wall, hands on his head. Perhaps I'm crazy, but I think he's doing it to protect me, not himself.

The tusk guys force me at gunpoint down the narrow metal-walled hall to an exam room. In one simple nanosecond, every single *National Enquirer* story I've ever read about alien abductions flashes through my mind. I can't get the words "anal probe" out of my mind. My body shivers in fear.

The room is stark. Robotic, high-tech machines straight out of a sci-fi movie are attached to the wall. The alien doctor is waiting for me. He's not wearing a white coat, just a navy-blue jumpsuit and the fakest, most smarmy smile I've ever encountered.

He's way more humanoid than the tusk people. He's human-sized, human-shaped, human in almost every way, except for the sky-blue skin. Slightly handsome, his face has those sunken cheeks and sharp blue eyes straight out of central casting for a generic movie villain of the good-looking variety.

"Hellooo," he says cheerily. "Now, who do we have here?"

I give him an icy stare. I refuse to make this easy for him. He wants a complete chart on me? Wants my medical history? Well, they should have thought of that before they beamed me aboard.

"A first name at least," he wheedles. "I'd hate to have to call you Patient C throughout the exam."

Icy stare. Feet planted. Maybe it's because we're alone in this room with no boar people, or that his collar controller is sitting on the counter a few steps away, but I feel emboldened

"Well, let's just get you up on the exam table." He pats it twice, decisively.

Angry glare, feet still planted, I imitate Zar's feral don't fuck-with-me look. What do you know? It works. His shoulders sag and his eyes inspect the floor. I get the distinct impression he doesn't want to be doing this any more than I do. His attitude is nothing like the aggressive, threatening guards.

"Look, Patient C, it is my job to ensure that intercourse and ejaculation have occurred in the proper, um, place. It will make it easier on both of us if you just," he pats the table again, twice in quick succession, "hop up here and let me take a quick look."

He has a speculum in hand and quacks it like a puppet mouth to emphasize the words, "quick look."

"You're a doctor? Where I come from doctors take an oath that says, 'above all do no harm.'" I give him the full force of my patented stink eye. "You went to school to be a doctor, a healer? And your mission on this ship is to examine my most private space to make sure the alien I've been forced to mate with has ejaculated in the correct hole? Really? You can go fuck yourself."

He looks at me, stricken. "Fuck? Myself?"

He's incredulous, obviously not understanding the idiom. My body hums with hope. I'm getting to him. Maybe there's no way to break out and pilot an alien spacecraft back to Earth, but perhaps I can connect with this guy. Maybe trigger his guilt and garner his help.

"Seriously, you went to years of school. Even though you're from a different culture, you had to have wanted to be a healer when you were younger, right? You're on a *slave ship*. You're double checking the culmination of *enforced rape*. You understand you're actively harming sentient beings, right? How do you look yourself in the mirror?"

Oh goodness, I really think I've gotten to him. His plastic happy look has completely evaporated, and his cheek muscle is twitching restlessly. He's silent for a long while, his face stony. "Let's get you up on the table." He's looking over my right shoulder, avoiding my eyes.

All right. I think I've pushed as far as I'd better go today if I want to stay alive. Perhaps, though, I've made him think.

After pulling off my pants, I hop up on the table. Although the doctor is blue and I'm on high alert, the procedure isn't any more uncomfortable than my annual exam back home. The entire assessment takes all of two minutes.

"The guards, the Urluts, will order you and your cellmate to have intercourse every day, and will bring you to me daily to confirm it. It would be much more pleasant for us both if you were to be more cooperative in the future." He gives a slight bow. Still avoiding eye contact, he lets me pull my clothes back on and escorts me to the door.

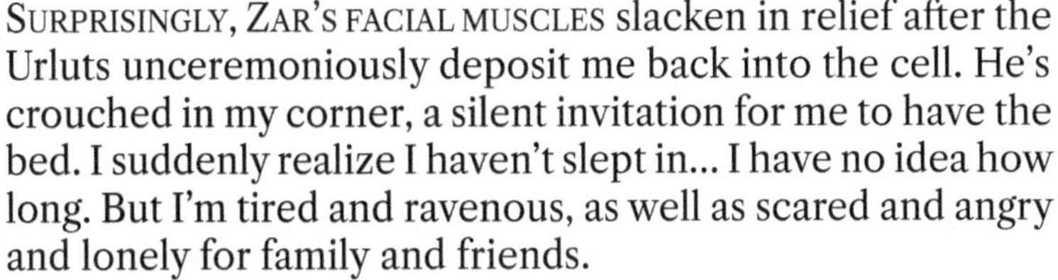

SURPRISINGLY, ZAR'S FACIAL MUSCLES slacken in relief after the Urluts unceremoniously deposit me back into the cell. He's crouched in my corner, a silent invitation for me to have the bed. I suddenly realize I haven't slept in... I have no idea how long. But I'm tired and ravenous, as well as scared and angry and lonely for family and friends.

I see some kind of food bars on the floor of the cell. They must have tossed them in when they brought me back. I grab them, drop half in Zar's lap, and plop on the bed.

"Are these edible?" I ask.

"They are nutritious, not delicious."

I doubt they rhyme in his language, but they do in mine and at the moment, sleep deprived and hungry, it strikes me as utterly hilarious. I laugh for at least a minute, feeling more and more insane as the seconds tick by, but I just can't stop giggling.

"You should eat, then sleep." He pauses for a long time, then he asks, sincere concern radiating from his golden eyes, "What did they do to you?"

"No anal probe," I say delightedly while waving my half-eaten bar, and then giggle some more. I can see by his unblinking expression he wants to know I'm okay, and my manic behavior is not reassuring him.

"Medical inspection to see we followed orders," I add more soberly.

He nods, his gaze skittering from mine. He probably suspected as much. It may be my first day in captivity, but it is certainly not his first time at the rodeo.

Zar

She wolfed down two food bars, opened the third, and fell asleep with it still in her hand. It's clearly been a long, grueling day for her. Is this feeling swirling in my belly empathy?

I don't want to wake her, but I can't sit here on the floor all night. We've already mated, so I don't imagine crawling into bed with her would terrify her. Moving over to the bunk, I gently slide in behind her, my back scraping the wall, then loosely hang my arm over her midsection. Before I lay my head on the mattress, I take a moment to observe her more closely.

At first, I'd found her flat face and beige flesh to be singularly unattractive. Now I see tiny variations on her skin with interesting little brown dots on her cheeks and nose. Her features seem soft and sweet, especially when she's sleeping. Short, light brown curls halo her face. Her pink mouth looked pretty when she smiled.

After settling my head on my bicep, I ponder why, after all the males and females I've been forced to couple with, I'm feeling intrigued by this female. I thought sexual attraction was yet another emotion I had shoved into the far recesses of my mind and completely locked away.

Clenching my jaw, I grind my teeth to try to turn off all thoughts and feelings. *Annums* ago I discovered emotional numbness is the best way to tolerate my captivity.

Anya

It's almost as if someone has called me awake from inside my head. The words, "Wake up," don't come through my ears. My eyes pop open and the first thing I'm aware of is Zar's warm, furred body wrapped around me like a second skin.

Outrage flares through me for half a second because his arm is slung intimately across my waist. Then I realize this bunk is tiny, and he has at least as much right to it as I do. He's taken no liberties, and truth be told, his soft warmth is reassuring.

Unable to shake the feeling I'm being stared at, I glance out the front of the cell to see an elf-like creature. She's three feet tall, maybe less. Her body appears lithe and graceful. Her eyes are uptilted and a shade of jade green so luminous they look lit from within. She has elf ears like in the movies—they're oblong and point up and back. She catches me looking at her and returns my glance expectantly.

I silently wonder if she's a prisoner or staff.

Prisoner. I hear inside my head.

You can hear my thoughts? I project the question toward her.

Yes, her voice, from inside my head, sounds as surprised as I feel.

Aliens, spaceships, lionmen and now this little elf talking in my ear? Wouldn't it be wonderful if someone slipped me some bad acid and this was just a dream?

No, this is real. Shaking myself fully awake, I remind myself job number one is to get back to Earth.

How come you have the run of the ship? I ask.

I'm the captain's pet. I'm so small and powerless they pay little attention. In exchange for favors, the captain gives me his protection.

If I wasn't cynical a day ago, I sure am now. A shiver slices through me as I wonder exactly what type of favors this little thing has to grant the male who captains this ship. Forcing that thought to the recesses of my mind, I say, *I'm Anya. Nice to meet you.*

Tyree.

Did you want something?

I just wanted to talk. I've never been able to have this kind of telepathy before. In the past, it's only been if someone asked, and wanted it, like the captain. I've never been able to wake someone out of a sound sleep before.

This is blowing my mind, I admit.

Me too.

Tell me, is there any way off this ship? Any way to escape? I want to barrage her with a hundred other questions, but I quiet those thoughts.

I've been a slave for a long time. On this ship for about one of your years. I have some ideas, but I don't think any would work.

Desperate, I pepper her with questions and learn a lot of useful information. It's clear she isn't any happier about being a slave than I am. She uses her budding powers of telepathy to cure the captain's anxiety and chronic insomnia. She stays in his room every night, lying on the floor at the foot of his bed, and soothes him to sleep with her abilities.

Because she's always been a model prisoner, she has the complete run of the ship. The guards treat her like she's of no more consequence than a potted plant. The captain keeps her on the bridge with him, where she calms him during the day.

Could you fly this ship? I ask boldly.

I've watched everything they do. I know a lot more than they suspect. But... I would never want to mislead you into thinking I could fly this ship on my own.

I'm sure she didn't need her powers of telepathy to read my dejection.

You __do__ want to escape? I ask.

Of course, I think all the slaves do. If it weren't for the collars, one of the batches of slaves they transport would have fought them a long time ago.

I'm not giving up, I tell her. *There's got to be a way out of here for all of us.*

The cell block door opens and Tyree scurries into the shadows as an Urlut stomps through the hallway doing a bed check.

With Tyree gone and nothing to distract me, I find my attention completely consumed by my proximity to my feline cellmate. His heavy, furred arm cradles my waist and his muscled front hugs my back.

I don't know what time it is, but my spidey senses tell me my bedmate has a severe case of "morning wood," because it's pressing insistently into the back of my thighs. He'll need that in a few hours when the Urluts will force us to "complete the act."

I drift back into an uneasy sleep with the words "surreal," and "lion-man," and "breeder" swirling through my dreams.

Zar

I'm rudely ejected from deep sleep to fully awake by the Urluts' loud commands to mate. They inform us that yesterday's abnormal one-day vacation from the *ludus,* our gladiator school, is over. They'll take us to the gymnasium to work out as soon as we complete our bed duties.

That suits me just fine. I didn't know what to do with myself yesterday with all that time on my hands. I'm used to lifting weights and sparring all day, every day. It's good that way—less time to think. And besides, I have absolutely nothing to say to this female.

Anya wakes with a groan, face tight, her gaze darting to remind her where she is. It's obvious the moment she recalls she's in captivity on a slave vessel. Her slight look of expectancy disappears, her brow wrinkles, and her lips tighten into a flat line.

I was born into captivity, at least as far back as I can remember. *Annums* ago, after many unsuccessful attempts to escape followed by painful consequences, I gave up any hope of freedom. Anya has had only one day to accept her new reality.

I can see by her tight muscles and angry eyes she desires no part of the Urluts' breeding program, nor does she want any part of me. I don't blame her. Neither of us wants anyone ordering us to share intimacy.

She walks to the toilet and gives me a scathing look, silently commanding me to look away. Her race must like privacy for that. I try to imagine a life where a person could have privacy for basic bodily functions. It must be nice.

Her cheeks already flushed with embarrassment, the color deepens as she shucks her pants and dives into bed. Covering her face with the blanket, she reaches between her legs and readies herself for me. I grab my length to stroke it, surprised to find it's already standing proud and ready to perform.

I wait for her hushed, "I'm ready," and join her under the blanket. She's on her hands and knees, as I'd instructed her yesterday, but I find myself yearning to mount her from the front, to see her interesting face and expressions. I'm certain that would distress her, so I just cover her from behind, and get ready to complete the act.

I'm certain she wants to get this over as quickly as I do, so I don't know what possesses me to touch one finger to her soft halo of brown curls or stroke her cheek with my knuckle. At first, she sucks in a breath and stiffens, but when I freeze and do nothing else, she calms herself, breathing more slowly, limbs relaxing.

I have no idea how to make this easier for her. Placing myself at her entrance, I notice her dampness there. I stroke the head of my cock back and forth, making sure she's slick enough to accept me. Gently placing my hands on hers, I reassure her wordlessly. I enter her slowly, tenderly, then finish the act as quickly as possible to cause her the least discomfort.

Anya

It's not that Zar and I have a relationship of any kind, but it hurts my feelings he can't stand to be inside me for more than thirty seconds. I should be happy he's so quick about his business. It's ridiculous for me to feel insulted—but I am.

Peeking at the women in the two cells I pass on my way to medbay, I give them my wordless support. I'm glad to see "boxer girl" in the cell next to mine is now wearing a humongous blue jumpsuit. I would have hated to have to walk around with my boobs exposed, especially with so many alien eyes watching every move.

The enforced sex hasn't been easy on any of us, but I think I heard her crying while "completing the act" this morning. I feel powerless realizing there's nothing I can do to help.

Paying little attention to anything but ideas of how to escape, I keep my pace brisk as an Urlut forces me down the hallways at gunpoint. While we hurry through the corridors, I notice every doorway and every turn as I look for crew I've never seen before.

If we were to stage a rebellion, we'll need to know the guard-to-prisoner ratio. I forbid myself to even wonder if the others want to overthrow our masters. Rather than being negative, I force myself to focus on escape.

Yesterday, I wasn't aware every male prisoner is a full-fledged, trained, powerful gladiator. Zar explained this morning that the only thing they do all day every day is train and fight. No wonder the Urluts are so quick to use shock collars on them. Even though the guards are huge and armed to the teeth, it sounds like they would be no match for any of these warriors if they squared off in a fair fight.

My thoughts come to a halt as we arrive at medbay. Dr. Evil, who never introduced himself even though he was so insistent I give him *my* name, tries to get me up on the exam table as fast as possible.

I decide to converse, even if it is one-sided, the whole time I'm in the exam room. I want him to realize he's hurting us women—that we're real people with emotions. Maybe I can reconnect him to his desire to be a helping professional.

"So, assuming at one point you wanted to heal people, what happened to you? How did you wind up serving on a slave ship?" How's that for getting right to the point?

He pats the table, looking resigned that I won't jump right up. We're having a stare-down. He sighs, shrugs, and for some unknown reason, answers me.

"Student loans."

"Say what?"

"You're right. I always wanted to be a physician, a healer. Medical training doesn't come cheap. I didn't want myself or my family burdened with my loans, so I accepted this job. It was supposed to be a quick one *annum* tour of duty with the Urluts on a transport freighter to erase all my debt.

"I was told I would tend the vessel's crew. I never dreamed the ship would transport slaves. Or that it would involve..." He looks forlornly down at the speculum in his hand as if it's the first time he's ever seen one. "It was bait and switch, but the contract is ironclad."

Those deep-set, piercing blue eyes look haunted for the briefest moment. Then he's patting the table again.

He paid the price for my cooperation today. After quickly shucking my PJ bottoms, I climb onto the table and slip my feet into the stirrups. How come they've invented space flight and they still can't figure out a way to warm those things?

"What are you going to do when you've paid your debt?" I ask afterward while I shrug into my clothes. I'm still trying to figure out how to use this information to my advantage.

"Originally, I thought I'd go back to Dacia, my home planet. But they could charge me with war crimes for this. They'll never allow me to return without harsh punishment."

Whoa, for being the one in total control of this situation, he certainly looks powerless and forlorn.

"I guess we're all prisoners in one way or another," I add faintly.

He breathes a deep sigh. We both know we'll be continuing this conversation tomorrow.

When I'm back in my cell, I have nothing to occupy my mind. I think it's been two days since I was kidnapped, but now my old life seems far away. I guess it *is* far away. I don't know much about space travel, but I'm guessing I could be millions of miles from Earth by now.

The call center where I worked has probably already sent me a termination notice via email for my two unexcused absences. Kinda makes me all warm and fuzzy inside, thinking about my relationship with my former employers. They didn't have shock collars at my job, but it felt like a master/slave relationship in other ways.

My fists ball in anger at myself. I hated that crappy job. Why was I sleepwalking through my life? How did my life get derailed? I had plans to go to college after I moved away from home. Instead, I accepted a shit job to ensure a steady income. Before I realized, several years passed and I never enrolled in business school. My plans for my future got hazier, and I got caught up in the treadmill of just getting by.

If I ever get back to Earth—like if this is a bad dream and I wake up any time soon—the first thing I'm going to do, if they haven't already fired me, is quit that soul-sucking job and find something I'm passionate about.

I wonder if my parents and two sisters know I'm AWOL. My chin trembles as I realize they must be worried sick. What I wouldn't give to Zoom with them right about now.

That's a depressing thought, which is doing me no good. I will not allow myself to fall down that rabbit hole. Switching gears, I nod my head in determination. I need to figure out how to escape.

We might have a chance. After all, we have a cadre of trained fighters who probably all want to be free. There's a ship's officer who hates what he's doing, and, of course, little telepathic Tyree.

After the guards transport us to medbay and back, they're pretty scarce. There doesn't seem to be a vast army of them on board, so they must be closely monitoring the gladiators and not bothering with us puny Earth women.

Gingerly fingering my shock collar, I decide to take a risk. Moving to the front of the cell next to boxer girl's compartment, I whisper, "What's your name?"

No answer. Also, no shock. So, emboldened, I ask more loudly.

"Shhhh," is her only reply. Then, after a moment while she's probably waiting to see if one of us gets zapped, she answers, "Grace."

"I'm Anya. It's nice to know your name. I was tired of calling you 'Boxer Girl' in my mind."

"I think of you as Moose," she admits with a soft laugh. "I'm glad the doctor got me these clothes, even though I look like the doc's Mini-Me in this rolled-up blue jumpsuit."

"Yes, I was glad to see that. It must have been awful for you to have to walk around almost naked that first day."

After pausing a moment while I wonder if I should mention my concerns, I barge ahead. "I've heard some... distressing noises from your cell. I've wondered if you've been crying. Is your guy treating you all right?" There is such a long silence I wonder if her collar's been shocked.

"It's awful," her voice is rough with emotion.

I'm not surprised. From the sounds of things, I'd wondered if the guy with the red robotic eye had been considerate with her during our mandatory mating.

"Grace, I'm so sorry. Does he understand he's scaring you? Hurting you?"

"He's... I'm not sure if he has actual emotions other than anger. We talk. When I told him it hurt, he slowed down. I think he tried. He warns me they'll punish us both if we don't follow orders. Maybe he thinks he's protecting me in some crazy way. I honestly don't think he wants to hurt me. He's just so... disconnected.

"I mean, have you seen his face? His arm? I'm not sure how much of him is human and how much is robot."

"I don't know how to help. Do you think my guy could talk to him at the *ludus* tomorrow? Urge him to be gentler? More considerate?"

"Anything's worth a try."

My head fills with selfish thoughts—like I'm so glad Zar has been kind. I try not to have any survivor's guilt over my luck.

Luck, that's a funny word to describe such an awful situation.

Chapter Three

ZAR

When I arrive back in the cell, I can't read Anya's human features. She's not shy about sharing, though.

"You've showered," she almost shouts. "So unfair! I'm dirty and stinky."

"Showered in the *ludus.*" I shrug my shoulders.

"I'm jealous. And filthy." She sniffs me. "You smell clean. And good."

I have no idea what to say, which is no problem because she always seems to fill the silences. But right now, she's wordless. She's staring at me like she's never seen me before. I smell something under her "filth," as she calls it. I smell... arousal.

Anya

He smells great. Not just clean, but a mixture of pine woods and musk. Then my mind goes straight to all kinds of crazy thoughts about my cellmate. I guess I was too busy to notice before, but he is sexy as hell.

He's rocking that angry feline vibe. His movements are so graceful as he paces around our little space. His mane, now clean, is eighties glam rock meets *Born Free*. The pronounced split between his flat nose and upper lip almost begs to be traced by yours truly. I imagine doing just that.

First with my finger, then with my tongue. *Stop it, Anya! What am I thinking?*

But his fur. How did I never notice how sexy it is? Soft fur covers his skin everywhere except his sex and tiny male nipples. I tried not to pay attention during our forced mating, but it feels like velvet.

My fingers itch to reach out and stroke him. I physically grip my thighs, where my hands are resting, to keep from investigating those rock-hard biceps.

This isn't right. I shouldn't be attracted to him. He's a different species FFS. It's just the enforced togetherness, right? I couldn't be aroused by this alien male. Could I?

But my heart beats faster and my palms get so clammy I have to rub them back and forth on my pajamas to dry them. My mouth is parched. My core clenches. I can't deny the desire welling up inside me.

I'll admit, it's been a long dry spell for me as far as males are concerned. Even though I sat on my ass all day at my job, there's something about the mind-numbing monotony of it all that made me so tired all I wanted to do when I got home at night was eat and watch Netflix. I've had my share of lackluster dates, but none that thrilled me. And none of them were as buff as the male standing a few feet in front of me.

I'm intently focused on how well-built Zar is. He works out all day, every day. His muscles are like corded steel ropes covered by soft golden suede. His fur accentuates his six-pack rather than obscuring it. And that loincloth leaves absolutely nothing to the imagination.

His eyes, those decidedly feline eyes, golden with black pupils, are compelling. Instead of his differences being scary or creepy, they are tempting as hell.

All at once, his appeal becomes obvious. I was so busy trying to ignore the forced bed sessions that I repressed my intense attraction.

Oops, he's staring at me. And by the looks of it, he has read my transparent little mind. And the result is not what one would expect from a hot, virile animal guy. Instead of acting on my obvious interest, he backs into the corner, slides down the wall, sits on his haunches, and begins to painstakingly study the floor, his tail lashing while the rest of his body is motionless.

This male could kill a grizzly with his bare hands, and I have completely debilitated him with my lustful looks.

He's not human. He's part animal. The way his nostrils are flaring, he probably smells my attraction. He's obviously not interested. Here we are, locked in this cell together. You'd think he'd take advantage of the situation—unless he finds me totally unattractive. My hands grip my elbows, and my stomach drops as I realize my feelings are hurt. I feel rejected.

Well, Anya, it's certainly not the first time you've had a crush that hasn't been reciprocated. It's just that this has made Zar extremely uncomfortable, and we have to live together in this tiny cell for the next who knows how long?

Should I just come out and acknowledge my faux pas? Ignore it? Deny it? Should I ask if he's gay?

"Um, I think I'm having a moment of temporary insanity." I ease onto the bed, completely flustered. After no response from him, I babble. "That's a legal term on Earth... it means you are not responsible for your actions. It can reduce the amount of punishment a person gets..." I trail off. I'm making it worse.

Zar

"Emotions are normal." Did I really say that? What a hypocrite I am. Well, they are normal, for everyone except me. Mine are nicely locked down, if they even exist at all.

"Is it hard for you?" she asks. "I mean being around almost-naked men all day and not being able to act on your attraction."

My confusion must show on my face because she elaborates.

"Are you gay?"

"I assure you, a lifetime of servitude has not made me happy."

She pauses, evidently searching for the right words. "I mean, are you attracted to other males?"

"No." I shake my head, my eyes narrowing. Why would she think that?

"Oh..." she stands still for a long time, then begins to slowly nod her head as if she's just solved a difficult puzzle. "You're just not attracted to *me*."

She looks dejected. I have no idea what to do. I'm not a talker. I'm not an explainer. I am not good with words. I'm a quiet male who has only had one actual relationship with another person his whole life.

I don't want to hurt her feelings. How do I explain I'm not a real person? I'm a stone who looks alive.

Her face is trembling. She's experiencing emotions. Lots of them. Bad ones.

"I have no attractions," I explain. "Not to males. Not to females. I wake, I fight, I eat, I sleep, and then I repeat."

She's watching me, wordless. "There's nothing in here." I lightly thump my chest. "I'm dead inside. I'm dead and my body just doesn't know it."

Tears well in her eyes. They quiver there for a moment and then two single tears slide down her cheeks.

"I didn't want to make you cry."

This somehow makes her cry harder.

I move without thinking. I'm instantly up on my feet, then I sit gently on the bed beside her—but not too close. She won't look at me. She's like a *lyrian* bug that rolls into a ball as its only defense.

"This isn't about you." My hand reaches up of its own volition to touch her, where, I do not know. It quickly drops back into my lap as if burned. She glances into my eyes and seems to calm a bit, so I keep gently talking.

"Your world has changed in an instant. You're scared and far from home. You just don't know what to do with all the feelings swirling inside you." I sound like I'm some expert on emotions, even though I have none.

Her tears are slowing. She's quietly gasping big gulps of air and giving me more eye contact. I think I've soothed her, at least a bit.

"You're right. I've been catapulted into a different universe. No one could remain completely sane after that, right?" she asks with a small, questioning smile and a sniff.

As quickly as the storm came, it has passed. Good. I think I've reached the limit of my ability to pretend to have or understand emotions.

I'm keenly aware of her thigh touching mine. I freeze and just pay attention to everything I'm conscious of. I breathe in deeply and smell her essence. She has a crisp, unique scent. It's intoxicating.

I'm paralyzed for a moment. Part of me, a large part, wants to rise from the bed and go back to my corner where it's safe and there are no demands on me.

But another part—a tiny undeveloped part—is sitting up straight inside, keenly interested in this developing connection shimmering between Anya and me.

Slowly, I find the courage to draw my gaze to hers. There is a spark of energy flickering through me. My heart pounds in fear, but I order myself not to look away. All the noises of the cell block cease. The sight of the drab gray walls recedes. All that exists in this vast universe are the two of us.

I reach out and touch her curls, surely the most courageous thing I've done in my entire life. I fight the urge to flee.

She doesn't move, just sits and maintains this delicious eye contact, savoring our intimate link.

My fingers slide through her hair. It's like silken springs. Then, my hand is on the back of her head. I pull her closer and lean toward her, unhurried. Finally breaking eye contact, I press my lips to hers. Sweet. There is no future, no past, just this moment of drowning in this female and this wondrous connection.

My lips feel hard on hers. Too hard. I soften the contact and her body responds instantly. Just soft lips against softer ones. Her shoulders relax. A sweet sigh escapes her.

I try to slow down. I don't want to scare her or push farther than she wants. The back of my mind knows it's kind of ridiculous to worry, considering we've already consummated things. But this, what's happening now, is different from what slaves are forced to do.

I could kiss her like this for *hoaras*, drowning in the intimacy of lips touching lips, but she presses at the seam of my mouth with her tongue. At first it shocks, then tickles, then it ignites a fire inside me. I open to her, and she sweetly invades my mouth. The tip of her tongue encounters the rasp of mine. I'm entranced by her soft slickness, and I wonder if she's equally fascinated by the gentle scrape of mine.

Her taste is intoxicating. There's no holding back. She is so open to me. Her little tongue wars with mine. Ah, a battle with no loser, only winners—I like this. Her hands finally leave her lap and clasp my shoulders. Her palms sweep to the back of my neck and tangle in my mane, pulling me even closer.

I'm besotted, not knowing whether to pay attention to the intimate battle our tongues are waging or the fact that her palms are now on my pecs, pressing on my muscles, her thumbs finding and gently flicking my nipples.

My cock kicks against its constraints, demanding release. Blood thrums insistently there, engorging, hardening. My tail wraps around her waist to press her even closer.

I tear my full attention back to my mouth and lips, our tongues. What's happening here is too delicious to hurry. I want to be fully immersed, memorize every *modicum*.

Pulling away just far enough, I nuzzle her cheek with mine. As I rub my scent onto her furless skin, I wonder at myself. It's a primitive impulse I've never felt before. After I give one more long stroke of my cheek against hers, obeying the need to mark my territory, I return to our kiss.

Our tongues spar. She thrusts, I parry. This is different than when we're forced to complete the act. This is voluntary. By choice. Her hands curl around my shoulders, sliding through my fur and pulling me even closer.

This time, she's the one who pulls away and nudges her cheek against mine, trying, I guess, to speak my language. Her attempt to bridge the barrier between us softens my heart and my tail tugs her tighter against me.

We return to our kiss, even more wholehearted. After nipping my bottom lip, she flicks her tongue against mine. When she encounters one of my fangs, she pulls back quickly, eyes widening. Her teeth are flat—she must not know how to navigate around my sharp canines.

"Don't worry," I croon, "I would never hurt you."

And then I'm gone. I've tumbled out of the present moment and down the deep well of time into the darkest part of my past. I'm eleven. Or at least I think I'm eleven. Born a slave, you don't exactly have anyone joyously celebrating your birthday. I'd been at the *ludus* my entire life and never had a meaningful relationship with another being.

One day, a new shipment of boys arrived. Like all newcomers, their fear was palpable. I could smell it. But the most amazing thing was that standing in the huddle of new males was another of my species. I'd never seen another of my species, but there he stood. We were so similar he could have been my brother.

I had only seen myself in a mirror once, but I could instantly identify another who looked like me. His fur was slightly darker than mine. His eyes were green as opposed to my golden ones. My muscles were better defined. But, yes, a stranger would have thought Pallatin and I were brothers.

I sat beside him at the first meal and introduced myself. After that, we were inseparable. We trained together, slept near each other's pallet on the floor, and helped protect each other from attacks by the older boys.

As much as we looked alike, we were so dissimilar in personality. I was strong and brash and angry. He was smart and deliberate and unsure of himself. I'd been raised a gladiator and had exercised, worked out, and sparred seven *hoaras* a day since I was old enough to understand language and follow instructions.

From birth, I was fed a scientifically formulated diet designed to put on muscle and no fat. My reflexes had been honed from *annums* of grappling, sometimes with males twice my age. Pallatin used to joke that I had eyes in the back of my head.

Pallatin was raised in a life that sounded like a storybook. I had trouble wrapping my mind around it. Loving parents, both a mother and father, raised him in a house where he had a bed in his own room with walls and a door. He ate what he wanted and described delicious foods I couldn't even imagine.

He attended a school where they didn't teach him fighting all day. They let him read books and learn about our world—the planet Ton'arr. It sounded wondrous to me. I admit I was sometimes jealous of his easy life and upbringing.

I was so interested in his books and his learning that he taught me the alphabet, then how to read and write. Learning new words excited me, stimulating a part of my mind that hadn't been tapped. We played during meals to see who could tally the most synonyms for everyday words.

Although he always won, he said I took to it quickly, but I felt clumsy and incompetent. He never derided me, though, and seemed genuinely pleased when I mastered something new.

Nor did I ever make fun of him in the *ludus*. He was slow and lumbering and did *not* have eyes in the back of his head. He had trouble striking with one arm while defending with the other. He didn't seem to even want to attack.

At night, after he'd taught me things about the universe, or the history of my people, the Ton'arr, I would gently coach him about his performance in the *ludus*. Perhaps he didn't understand that what he taught me was interesting, but not important. What I taught him could one day save his life.

Before I met Pallatin, I'm sure I'd heard the laughter of others. As I think about it now, most of that laughter was derisive, making fun of others' misfortune or loss. Being raised in slavery does not bring out anyone's higher purpose or better instincts.

I'd never actually laughed before he arrived. He told me a pun once that was so funny I burst out laughing. I had never heard a joke before. I was shocked to hear a bark of laughter escape my mouth.

After that, I begged him to tell me more. He couldn't. He told me he didn't have many jokes memorized. So we began to make things up, silly things, ridiculous stories, anything that would bring even a small smile to our lips. Before him, I had been an automaton. Pallatin introduced me to my soul.

It was the best time of my life—to know someone had my back and that one other being in the galaxy cared whether I lived or died. Another person was interested in the thoughts flying through my head. He listened to my opinions and cared about my emotions. It was a completely new experience. Those were heady times.

He hadn't been at the *ludus* quite an *annum* when one day we were issued new loincloths—never a good omen. It meant someone had come from off-world interested in either a show or to purchase one of us.

Can'an, the head gladiator, looked thunderously angry when he strode into our quarters that morning, clutching his clipboard so hard his knuckles were white.

"There will be two contests today, a spectacle for off-worlders. The docket has already been decided. Annot and Guarmond will fight first." Can'an's face squeezed in some emotion I couldn't read. "Zar and Pallatin, you are matched second." A long pause. "To the death," spoken so low I almost couldn't hear it.

I could swear my heart stopped beating. Surely this couldn't be true. I had never heard of anyone under fifteen fighting in a match to the death. And had only heard of one match of fifteen-*annum*-olds, which was punishment for an escape attempt.

I knew the masters and owners didn't care about the ethics of fighting sentient beings to the death. They treated us cavalierly. So many times I had heard of a master who was down on their luck but not ready to sell, who would put his fighters on half rations without recognizing we athletes need to be at peak performance to save our very lives.

I'd seen every callous behavior that could be imagined perpetrated on my peers, but I had always counted on our owners' greed to keep us alive for at least several more *annums*. It wasn't cheap to acquire fighters. Nor was it inexpensive to feed, train, house, or keep us healthy enough to fight. Killing us just didn't make financial sense.

But I knew I'd heard Can'an correctly, because the look on Pallatin's face must have matched my own. His jaw hung loose, his eyes widened, his shoulders slumped.

"Surely this can't be true," I spoke up. "You must know this is not a fair match!" What a pitiful argument it was then. It sounds hollow to this very day.

Can'an's teeth clenched. He didn't respond. I realized later that he, a former gladiator himself yet still a slave, must have dreaded delivering this news almost as much as we hated receiving it.

"One *hoara* from now, in the ring," was all the teacher said, his jaw tight. He then turned on his heel and left our barracks.

Pandemonium rang out, all the young males talking at the same time. They were angry, shocked, and afraid, but Pallatin and I only wanted each other's company. We went to a corner and stood, my hands on his young shoulders, his on mine.

There was no use trying not to cry, Pallatin was already doing so. We both knew he was no match for me. We both knew who would die in an *hoara* and we were powerless to do anything about it.

"I won't do it," I announced stubbornly. "They'll have to kill us both."

"No, my friend. Only one of us needs to die today."

"I can't do it. I can't..." I couldn't see anymore. Tears clouded my vision.

"We are slaves, Zar. We live and die at their mercy. I must die today."

To this day, I will never know how he found such courage and wisdom.

"We must give them a show, draw it out. I know you could finish me in thirty *modicums*, but perhaps whoever is paying for this spectacle will appreciate your prowess, buy you, and take you from this hellhole."

"This hell hole or another, what does it matter? You're the only thing that makes life bearable."

"Stay strong," he said, even though he had to be shattering inside. "Promise me two things..." He paused until I nodded. "When it is time, do it swiftly."

"Of course." I still die a little when I remember this conversation. It breaks my heart to think the greatest gift I could give my best friend was a quick death.

"And second," he waited for me to look into his piercing stare, "do not take responsibility for my death upon your heart. It may be your hand that holds the sword, but it is upon their order."

How could a twelve-*annum*-old be so wise? Or so wrong. To this day, I have never been able to follow his last wish. I've never forgiven myself.

I watch our final match in my mind's eye, seeing every blow, hearing every raucous cry from the stands, smelling the coppery scent of my best friend's blood, and reliving down to the most minute detail the depths of my pain, grief, and guilt.

And then the memory comes to a halt. The metallic smell of my cell block intrudes. I'm aware of my thighs on the bed. Opening my eyes, I come back to the present, sitting still as a statue. I focus on my breathing. It's the only thing I can bear to pay attention to.

I would do best to leave the human alone. I don't know what possessed me when I told her I would never hurt her. What a lie! All I do is hurt every single being I touch. I kill people who care about me.

I walk to the back corner of the cell and slide down the wall until I'm squatting on the floor. I'll sleep here tonight. I will not share my bed with the female until the next order to mate and that will be from behind. As quickly as possible.

I go away. Disappear. I'm not in pain. I simply don't exist.

Anya

Squatting in the corner, even his tail limp on the floor, he's still as a marble sculpture. If that statue had a name, it would be "Agony."

I may not have an advanced degree in psychology, but I think my cellmate has a definite case of PTSD. I can't think of any explanation other than a heart attack that could pull someone so completely out of such a sensual embrace.

One second, he's kissing me like I've never been kissed before. The next, he promises to never hurt me, then he pulls back, closes his eyes, and when he opens them, there is a world of pain before it shuts off and he moves to the corner of the cell.

His face is a mask of total despair. I have no idea where his thoughts went, but his look of anguished misery speaks volumes. This large Atlas of a man is so fragile at this moment I just want to reassure him—but I don't know how.

In my twenty-five years on Earth, I've never been at such a clear choice point. I could sit on the bed and dive into my misery. I could count all the things I miss, from cotton-soft clouds in the blue sky to my favorite song, to my friends and family. Or I could get my ass over to the corner and connect with the male in this cell who has tried very hard to make this as easy as possible for me, and who is lost in his internal torment.

I walk to the corner, slide my back down the wall next to him until we are hip to hip squatting on the floor. He's motionless and paralyzed—that's okay. It gives me time to wallow in all the things I miss. That soon gets maudlin and boring.

My thoughts veer to the aborted kiss we shared. I touch the pads of my fingers to my lips as I relive those quick, intense moments. I've never experienced that level of arousal from just a kiss before. I don't think it was simply because of the amazing, rough burrs on his tongue. We were sharing a connection.

I might not want to admit it, but I'm becoming more captivated by him every day. There's a tempting combination of rough strength and gentle vulnerability I find hard to resist. Sadly, though, he might be too damaged to return the attraction.

Chapter Four

ANYA

I'm abruptly awakened from a sound sleep the next morning with the order to "complete the act." It's actually a blessing to startle straight awake into the bleak reality of my existence, rather than come slowly out of a sweet dream, still believing I'm in my own bed back on Earth. Nope, I'd rather wake right up to the grim reality of my life.

I'm not still cramped in the corner on the floor next to Zar. I dimly remember him carrying me to bed in the middle of the night. As I slept, my back burrowed snugly against his warm front, his arm gently braced across my stomach to keep me from falling off the tiny mattress.

I flip around so we're front to front and catch him looking at me. For a moment, he doesn't appear to be a statue at all. He seems tender, his gaze is gilded and warm. Then I can almost hear the clang of his emotions slamming down and he is stone again.

He slides along the wall to the end of the mattress, then stands at the back of the bed. I shuck my bottoms, assume the hands and knees position under the covers, and truly understand Zar's dead eyes for the first time. He's had to do things like this his whole life. I'm only on my third day and I'm feeling my humanity and all hope slip from my grasp.

I'm not sure it was even possible, but Minute Man was quicker about his business than previously.

We only have a few minutes before one of us is dragged off at gunpoint, but I need to talk to him about Grace.

I lower my voice, not wanting to embarrass her. "Zar, have you noticed..." How do I approach this? For all I know, he and Grace's guy are besties. "Have you heard the female in the next cell crying?"

"I wondered if that was what I was hearing."

Okay, good, he's talking to me, even if he's giving me zero eye contact. Talking is better than the silent treatment.

"I spoke with her yesterday and she says her guy is rough." He gives me a questioning glance. "You know, rough in the mornings..." I wait until understanding dawns on his handsome face. "You guys are big. It takes some finesse."

He nods slowly. "I'll speak with him. He can be brash and thoughtless sometimes. I understand this hasn't been easy for any of you females."

Although he didn't say it, it's clear this hasn't been easy for him, either.

The Urluts appear and I'm unceremoniously marched to medbay by tusky, hairy boars.

Dr. Evil looks tired and defeated.

"It's awfully early in the morning to be so tired," I jab, not understanding why I always needle him. Maybe because I'm so powerless in every other way and, for some reason, this male doesn't fight back.

"You're not going to get to me today, Patient C," he chides, waggling his finger as he feigns cheeriness.

"'If you're not part of the solution, you're part of the problem.'" I throw at him. "It's an Earth quote."

No response. I'm still hopeful I can trigger his compassion—or maybe his guilt—and convince him to help us somehow.

"'If you're neutral in situations of injustice, you have chosen the side of the oppressor.' That's a quote from Earth's great oracle, Facebook."

"I'm just doing my job," he defends, his blue gaze full of sincerity.

Ohhh, can I explain the backstory of the Nazis and the Nuremberg trials? I have no time for that. "Some bad people on Earth were sentenced to death for using that as an excuse."

He looks stricken. "Really?"

"Yeah. Death sentences. A lot of them. 'Just following orders' is not an acceptable justification."

"Table." He pats it with his palm, then grabs the speculum.

I realize I'm getting no joy from our usual banter, so I hop on the table and assume the position. Ninety seconds later, my feet hit the floor, the procedure finished. "Is there a shower around here? I could be done in less than three Earth minutes. Promise."

He sighs, his eyes flicking to a door at the other end of the exam room. "No more than three *minimas*, C. Shampoo is in the green bottle."

When I'm back in my cell, I'm not surprised that Zar is gone. Not that I'd enjoy "gladiatoring" all day, but I do envy that he has something to do. Sitting in this 8x8 cell all day sucks the life right out of me.

I step to the front of the cell and stage whisper for Boxer Girl, I mean Grace. "Hey, Grace, I spoke with Zar. He's going to talk to your cellmate today. Are things any better?"

"When I asked, he told me his name. He's called Shadow. But otherwise, nothing's changed."

Although my cheeks burn in embarrassment, I offer this handy little piece of advice, "When the Urluts make the announcement, you might want to um, prepare yourself for him." When there's no response, I wonder if I need to elaborate.

"Yeah, I figured that out after the first day," she finally chimes in, probably as bashful as I am.

"He won't talk to you at all?"

"No, not really."

"Could you see how he feels about escaping? Would he be open to fighting for our freedom?"

"I have no idea."

"The Urluts look so much alike, but I think I can tell them apart. I've seen four of them, plus the captain and the doc. Probably some more, but there couldn't be that many. There are ten gladiators. We've got them outnumbered if everyone is willing to fight. Talk to Shadow."

Long silence. "I'll try, but he's kind of a dead man walking."

"Boy, that sounds familiar. Zar, too. We'll be like that in time, probably soon, when we're just burned-out hopeless husks. We've got to escape, and soon."

"Okay, I'll talk to him. Not promising anything, though."

I decide to exercise for a while. I'm not sure that five minutes of running in place is going to do much to prepare me for the upcoming battle, but it allows me to feel productive.

I start panting after maybe three minutes but console myself with the thought that maybe it's the high altitude that's making me so out of breath. High altitude—that thought makes me giggle. Then I have nothing to do but lie here and worry.

Anya! Anya, can you hear me?

It's Tyree. In my mind. I bolt upright, looking for her. It's surprising she'd be bold enough to sneak into this area during the day when all the lights are on. There's no sign of her, though.

Yes, I hear you. Where are you?

I'm on the bridge, sitting at the captain's feet.

Cool. I thought you said you weren't very good at this. You're getting more powerful.

I've been trying to reach you this way since we last spoke. It's like a muscle that keeps getting stronger. But today it's urgent. The captain was discussing the flight plan with his first mate.

Oh, mental note, add first mate to the list of people we have to kill.

Yes?

We arrive on Hyperion in eight days. It's a notorious planet, known for its gladiator fights, slave auctions, and sex workers. They were talking about the um... breeding. They just threw random males and females together to see if they could easily get any of you pregnant. You will fetch higher prices if you carry a young. You know, two for one. But no one who is on Hyperion to buy slaves—or livestock as we're considered—will care if you're mated or not.

You'll be sold to the highest bidder. You and Zar will be separated. I don't know if that matters to you or not. But that's what will happen.

I swallow repeatedly as I ponder this information for a moment and honestly don't know how I feel about any of it, especially the idea of being separated from Zar. My mind still gets stuck on the pregnant part. I'm not on any birth control, but I can't fathom that possibility.

If we're going to break out, Tyree continues, *it had better be before we're in orbit around that planet. When we get there, things will move fast. Slavery is legal in most parts of the known galaxy, but abduction from primitive planets that don't have spaceflight is not. All you females are illegal. Captain Gren will want to sell you quickly, make some easy credits, and dash into hyperspace before the authorities are any wiser.*

I sigh heavily and wonder if she can "hear" it.

Crap. So we have seven days. My mind is processing like the world's fastest computer as I crunch through as many angles as I can think of. I have no new and brilliant thoughts on how to overthrow this crew, but I certainly don't want to be sold into a different kind of slavery on Hyperion.

As I see it, I continue, *we have two major problems. The biggest of which are these delightful collars. We can't take the first step if the collars are still activated. We'd all be dead before we're one minute into the escape.*

And the second?

The captain. I'm sure none of us knows how to fly this ship. How do we subdue him enough to force him to fly this ship?

There's a long silence, and then it's almost as if her voice lowers and she's whispering in my mind.

You know why he keeps me around, right? I crawl into the captain's mind and lull him to sleep at night. What if I can get into his brain to make him do other things against his will? If I can do it without him catching on, perhaps I'm strong enough to get him to turn off the collars and then maybe fly this vessel. Let me try a few things.

Watch yourself, Tyree. If he catches on to what you're doing, he might kill you.

Zar

As I'm escorted back to my cell with my comrades, I'm filled with dread at seeing Anya. I have no idea why she sat next to me on the cold, hard floor last night rather than lie down on the bed. I sense she wants something from me. My nostrils flare in anger as my tail slashes. Doesn't she realize I have nothing to give?

As the guards open my cell, I see her sit upright on the bed. If I'm not mistaken, she seems glad to see me, happily expectant. I must not understand human emotions—she couldn't want to see me. I can't believe she'd even want to look at me after all we've been forced to do together.

She looks so beautiful. Her brown hair is clean and shiny. The smell she calls filth is gone, and I breathe in her personal scent. My cock takes notice, twitching in my loincloth. Never before have I been attracted to anyone I've been forced to couple with, which is lucky.

I've had no connection to anyone since Pallatin. I remind myself the last thing I need to do is get attached to another living thing.

After picking up the food bars the guards threw on the floor, I toss half to her. She hands me half of her half.

"You need more than I do to survive," she offers.

"You have to keep up your strength, too."

"You're twice as big as me and you work out all day. I'm right, you're wrong. Let's never have this argument again, okay?" Her jaw is set in determination as she spears me with a hard gaze.

I nod and accept the food, then turn around to look at the gray wall so she can't read my surprise. Not even Pallatin would have given me his portion of food. It's everyone for himself in this world. Her behavior makes no sense. I simply can't understand it.

She pats the bed next to her, and I join her there. She tells me about the little female I've seen sneaking around the cellblock and their ability to speak mind to mind.

"Tyree says we'll arrive on Hyperion in eight days," she whispers. "If we're to escape, we have seven days to do it."

"Anya, I've been captive, a slave, all my life. There is no escape. You shouldn't get your hopes up. It will demoralize you even more when you realize how powerless you are. There's a zero chance of your plan working. You realize that, right?"

"We have ten gladiators, right?"

My words didn't even faze her. I nod dumbly.

"I'm thinking that the attack will have to start when the males are in the *ludus* and have access to weapons. What weapons do you have there?"

I realize there's no reason to argue, she'll just keep pushing for answers. I sigh. "They keep the weapons heavily locked. Behind the sealed door are wooden swords, lances, tridents, bows, and blunt-tipped arrows as well as large nets to disable the opponent."

"Holy fuck. They have lasers, electronic collars, and sophisticated killing machines and our side has wooden swords..."

She looks completely dejected. I can see hope spooling out of her, her facial muscles loosening, her shoulders sagging.

I know it's ridiculous, but I jump in, trying to give her something to believe in. "Only two guards watch us. There are ten of us and two of them. We're trained warriors and might be able to overpower them. It's just that the collars..."

"We might have a workaround for the collars."

She explains more about Tyree and her abilities, making sure to keep her voice low, next to my ear.

"Okay... let's just say that by this mental magic your friend can get the captain of the ship to disable the collars." I can't hide the dubious tone of my voice. "We rush the guards, overpower and kill them, take their weapons—they have three each. That gives ten gladiators six weapons and the passkeys to most places on the ship. We leave the *ludus* and work our way to the bridge, killing any overseers along the way. Let's assume another miracle happens and we can just barge onto the bridge. Then what?"

"These are good questions. We have to get the strategy right. I have so much intel to gather."

Her jaw is firm, eyes focused on the ceiling while she ponders. As I'm running various escape scenarios in my head, I'm thoroughly distracted by the delicate curve of her throat. Sometimes her beauty strikes me completely out of nowhere, surprising me as it does right now. But it's not just how she looks that attracts me—it's her hope, her determination, her strength.

"Tyree can help me figure out exactly how many people are on this ship, what their jobs are, and where they are when the gladiators are in the *ludus.* Seriously, Zar, I know ten gladiators can overpower the two guards. With laser weapons, your contingent has a good chance against the others. And every additional guard you kill probably nets you one or two more weapons. I think we just might pull this off."

I nod as she speaks, feeling a lightness of spirit I haven't felt since Pallatin made me laugh. Could this be... hope?

No. I can't allow this. I won't dash her little dream of escape—that would be cruel. But I can't allow myself to share in her delusion—that would be stupid.

Anya

He looks so skeptical. I mean, I think it's taking everything he has not to scoff at me.

My racing thoughts of escape are hijacked by how handsome he is. I was never really attracted to the perfect movie star fantasy of male perfection. In the past, I've been tempted not only by the antisocial bad boy—come on, who hasn't?—but also the occasional distracted computer geek as well.

I like different, and boy does Zar qualify. I'm also drawn to his quiet strength. Perhaps I'm crazy, but I feel something developing between us. I enjoy his company and look forward to his return from the *ludus* every day. I sigh heavily. I don't know how I feel about him.

We're still sitting on the bed. My feet are dangling off the edge, his flat on the floor. "Did you talk to Shadow?"

He nods, frowning a little. "Shadow is..." He struggles to find the words. "Like me, Shadow learned to cut himself off from his feelings. I don't think he realizes he's being harsh or rough. I think he believes he's doing her a favor. You know, getting the mating accomplished so they don't punish her."

I cock my head, not understanding what is so freaking hard to comprehend about physically hurting someone or wanting to be tender.

"I explained things to him. He's not stupid. I believe he'll try harder to... be gentle."

Reaching out, I touch Zar's arm. I'm slow and soft, not wanting to trigger another disappearing act like yesterday. I just want to connect with him, not have sex.

"So how'd *you* do it? You cut yourself off from your feelings just like Shadow did. But you seem hyperaware of being gentle. You've both been hurt. How is it that, although you've both been through so much, you respond so differently from each other?"

Zar

"I don't know," I hedge. I'm not good at this—talking and examining myself and my emotions. I've spent my whole life avoiding those things. Why is this female so full of *dracking* questions?

But I try. I try to search myself. It feels important to Anya, so perhaps it should be important to me.

Like a bolt of lightning, I realize I do know why we're different. It's obvious why I'm "hyperaware" as Anya called it. Now I have to decide if I want to divulge it to her.

I know what Anya sees when she looks at me. She pays attention to my body. I smell her arousal. I think she likes the way I'm built. Looking at her musculature, I can only imagine I'm bigger and stronger than males of her species. I'm pretty sure she's attracted to my brawn.

If I tell her why I'm so capable of tuning in to her feelings, I'm pretty sure it will repel her. Part of me doesn't want to disgust her. That part wants her to be drawn to me, excited by me, to admire my power.

But another part realizes it would be easier for both of us if I repulsed her. If I disgust her, then maybe this ridiculous, unhealthy, destructive attraction would end. Severing this bond would benefit us both. It would kill this dangerous hope building in my breast. It would make it easier for her when we're separated on Hyperion—a fate that is all but guaranteed.

Before I can second guess my decision, I decide to tell her the truth. It will instantly kill her interest.

"I know what it's like to be raped." There, it's out. I want to annihilate what's between us. I want to scorch the soil so nothing can spring back up between us again. I'll tell her even more details. I'll keep talking until she can never look at me the same way. I'll tell her things she'll never be able to forget, images in her mind she'll never be able to unsee.

"I know what it's like to have things forced on me. My owners have sold me for the night, sold me for days and weeks and even *lunars*. They forced me to pleasure males and females and couples. I've been forced to be the receiver and the giver. I've been tied down..."

"Please Zar, that's enough."

"No, it's not enough, Anya. Don't you want to know more?" I have no idea why I feel the need to continue. It's like going in for the kill in the arena. I've never enjoyed that part of what I've been forced to do, but now I can't stop. I must slay the attraction between us. Slay it with my words.

"I've been forced to..."

"Please stop! Please." She's begging.

I find the courage to glance at her. She's shocked, I can tell. She's not even trying to keep her face blank. She's in pain. If I read her correctly, she's in misery. Maybe I'll be lucky and she'll stop with the questions and leave me alone.

She turns toward me, bending her knee, which grazes my thigh so she has a better angle to see me. She leans slightly toward me, captures my face in her palms, and simply holds my gaze with hers.

Thankfully, she's silent. No words, no questions, no platitudes. She simply shares the silence with me. I thought I'd be embarrassed after revealing my past. No woman wants her male to be weak. What I just admitted to her exposed the depth of my deficiencies.

Her gaze penetrates mine, down to my soul. It doesn't appear she's thinking I'm weak. I feel her compassion. Any disgust or contempt? No, that's completely absent.

I search down into myself, assessing what I'm feeling. I was calculated. I wanted her to be repulsed. So why? Why is she giving me compassion instead? My mind betrays me. My thoughts tell me she pities me. I want to hate her for that.

But I know it's not pity. It's empathy, tenderness, connection. I can't fight it anymore. I dig deep to find the courage to attempt to let it in. I try to allow it to wash over me. For a moment, I permit myself to feel it. I'm being drenched in her warm benevolence. It touches my heart. I feel warm and not completely alone for the first time since Pallatin. And this is a million times bigger than what I felt with him.

Then I shift my gaze and pull out of her grasp. I shut things down. I could drown in Anya's gentle affection if I let myself. I can't allow that. It's far more dangerous than the arena.

Chapter Five

ANYA

The next morning before the Urluts wake us, I flip over to face Zar in an effort to get comfortable, only to catch him looking at me. He instantly closes his eyes.

That warm look in his golden gaze grips my heart.

"Are you pretending to sleep?" I tease. He's so busted.

"Mmm," he answers noncommittally, but his feline eyes open and look calmly at me.

There is so much unsaid between us, so much we need to discuss. Last night was a revelation in so many ways. This powerful alien has fault lines in his toughness—cracks of vulnerability. I doubt we will ever discuss what he shared with me last night. I wonder if he regrets disclosing what he did. Well, no matter, we're kind of stuck with each other. We've got to put all that behind us. I will certainly never mention it again.

"You are so handsome." That just slipped out. That's one way to avoid the elephant in the room.

His eyes widen in astonishment.

"You're surprised I think you're handsome?"

He pauses a moment like I've caught him in some trap and he's trying to figure out a way to answer, "does my ass look fat in these pants?" without pissing me off.

"I'm so different from you. I'm shocked you find my features pleasant."

Comprehension slowly dawns on me. That one statement allows everything to click into place like tumblers on a safe. I'm sure my face shows all the emotions rolling through me, from embarrassment to sadness to anger. "So that's why you don't find me attractive? I'm so different from you?" I'm not sure I want to hear his answer, but I keep my eyes glued to his.

His eyebrows slash down. He truly looks bewildered. "Why do you think I don't find you attractive?"

"Ummm, because you can't bear to look at me when you're fucking me? You insist I get on all fours. Because you obviously work hard to be inside me the absolute minimum amount of time?"

I hadn't noticed, but his hand has been gently stroking my hair. That slight touch is so comforting, so tender.

His jaw is working, as if he's going to say something, but wants to make sure he says the exact right thing. "I think you're beautiful, Anya." His gaze is still piercing into mine. "You're the most beautiful thing I've ever seen." His gaze darts away, as if that was hard to say.

"Really?" I let his words wash over me. When they fully register, it feels incredible. Every cell in my body relaxes.

"Yes." He's playing with my hair, smoothing his palm over my forehead, tracing his fingertips butterfly-soft down my cheek to my jaw. His gaze is still locked on mine. He's not lying, he's totally sincere.

"Then why do you insist on doggy style? Why can't you wait to get 'the act' over?"

He sighs, his brows compressed in confusion. "I did it for you."

"For me? Do Ton'arr women not enjoy sex?"

"I've never met a Ton'arr woman. I wouldn't know." A muscle leaps on his lower right jaw. His face clouds. The hand in my hair stills.

"What do you mean you did it for me?" my tone is softer now.

"Because that's what helped me... tolerate it. It helped me keep whatever semblance of dignity I managed to maintain." Such a long pause. I detect the briefest passing moment of grief before he pulls the curtain down over his emotions. "Not having to look at the other person... keeping it brief... those things helped me keep a hold on to who I was when I was being violated. Being quick... no eye contact, was my attempt to make it easier for you." His eyes seal closed and I get the feeling he's not here with me anymore.

My brain entirely disengages for a moment. My eyes fill with tears. Zar is just a blur. Oh shit. He's been through so much, this gorgeous gladiator who's built of granite. He's endured kidnap, beatings, rape, yet his kindness to me has never faltered.

My heart clenches in my chest. I ache for him. I see him as a little boy so clearly in my mind's eye I can almost smell and hear it. That hurt little boy still resides in the colossal, muscular male lying next to me.

I reach out with one finger and softly draw a line from where his mane borders his forehead, down the middle of his flat, feline nose, hovering at the cleft above his mouth. His eyes are still closed. He must be mortified after what he's shared.

I press my palm gently to his cheek and he leans into it with a tiny, shuddering sigh. Although he must feel shame deeply, I think he yearns for my closeness, my touch.

"After just these last few days, I now totally understand that we all must do what we have to do to survive. People can imagine how they might handle things if bad stuff happens, but no one knows how they'll feel or what they'll do until that moment comes. My moment came when they threatened to kill me if I didn't mate with you, and I couldn't move fast enough to comply. I chose life, Zar. I still choose life."

He's looking at me now, allowing the intimacy of eye contact. His muscles are tight, he's leaning in. He's hanging on every word—he wants to believe me.

"Someone can throw mud on me, but that doesn't make me dirty. Not as long as I feel clean. I feel clean about what you and I have done in this bed. I think you should feel clean about what they forced you to endure, too. Clean and strong, Zar.

"No matter how many muscles you have, how many opponents you've killed in the arena, you can't fight the collar. I admire you. I think you're amazing and strong and you've done the absolute best you can. You're extraordinary, Zar."

He takes a moment, his breathing becoming less ragged, and then he pierces me with the most beautiful and poignant gaze I've ever received. The impenetrable walls he keeps between us crumble.

In this moment, his past is gone, my past is gone—there is only now. We are fully connected. I feel my heart open to him like the petals of a flower. I've never shared a connection as deep and meaningful as what I'm feeling now.

He leans in to kiss me, and all his previous reluctance has vanished. Now he is the prowling predator he resembles. His golden eyes seem to glow from within. His kiss is soft, yet forceful—close-lipped kisses all over my cheeks, forehead, and eyelids. Then gently on my mouth until he presses his tongue against the seam of my lips.

I open to him immediately. I've wanted this for days. Without stopping for breath, he moves on top of me, knees straddling my hips. I love the sharp rasp of his feline tongue on mine as he plunders my mouth. One hand cradles my head. He's in full control. I couldn't escape if I wanted to.

Our tongues dance, his penetrating my mouth, then retreating to lick my lips. He presses back in as if to savor me more fully. He moans softly in the back of his throat as if my taste is divine and he can't get enough of me. His weight is fully on his knees, and yet his big body enveloping me feels wonderful. I feel precious and small in his leonine embrace.

My body is completely alive, on fire with need. His cock, huge and engorged, presses against my core. My arousal is dripping through my folds, my clit pulsing with need. Part of me wants him to enter me right this moment, while another part wants this desperate urgency to build even higher.

He nuzzles my neck with tiny nips of sharp fangs. Between that and his warm breath fanning my skin, I'm spinning in a haze of desire. My channel clenches with need.

He pulls off my top, and his eyes narrow in appreciation as he lets loose a throaty growl. I've never felt as though I was a package being unwrapped before. But he acts as if this is the most precious present he's ever received.

"So beautiful," he breathes, then just admires my body with his scorching gaze. His gentle finger circles my nipple as his tail wraps around my ankle. Is he aware I'm on fire? He's teasing me on purpose and building heat along every synapse, every fiber of my being.

Leaning his maned head down, he sighs. His warm, humid breath flows across my throat, fueling my excitement even higher. My pebbled tips, already well beyond aroused, are aching for more. Finally, he tongues my nipple.

I've always loved this part of foreplay, but dear God, the rasps of his feline tongue on my sensitive bud could totally project me through the roof. I'm trying to be quiet because of the complete lack of privacy on the cell block, but holy shit, it's all I can do not to moan and beg and make weird mewling animal noises in the back of my throat. I settle for throwing my head back against the mattress and zoning in on the desire building between my legs.

"You like this, Anya? My tongue?" he rasps.

I scrape my nails up and down his back in answer. His fur is soft and sensual. The tactile feeling is foreign, exciting.

He moves to my other breast, scraping just the tip of the nipple with his abrasive tongue. I'm right on the edge of pleasure and the tiniest bit of pain. If he stops, I will simply die. But I need him to stop what he's doing so he can finally fill me with his gorgeous cock. I am burning with hunger. I hear my breathing coming in labored pants.

He sleeps nude, just muscles and warm, soft, golden fur. I have my panties and flannel bottoms on. I'm already drenched. My hips are involuntarily thrusting to get more delicious friction. His thick cock rides the outside of my clothes in an exquisite rhythm, and I'm lost in the sensation.

He pulls back for a moment and tugs my bottoms off, but leaves the panties on. He pulls the panties up almost to the ripping point and the pressure of the silky fabric against my clit pumps my desire up a notch. I suck in a harsh gasp of breath, my eyes widening.

No longer a sentient being, I am functioning totally on impulse. My thoughts are gone. I'm in an exquisite haze of feeling and need.

I'm raking his back with my fingernails, harder now—silent code for more. He sits up and in an instant, he drags my panties off and tosses them aside. He growls low in his throat as he spreads my legs, my knees falling to the sides in open invitation.

"How could you have wondered for a moment that I don't think you're beautiful?" he whispers, his voice deep and gravelly. He moves his knees between my legs, leaning over me and breathing in my ear. "The Gods were generous when they threw you in my cell."

"Zar, please," I urge him frantically, pulling him against me and pressing fiercely with my heel on his firm, muscled ass.

He cups my cheeks with his palms, giving me a look that tells me I'm precious, and then he rides me. His enormous cock presses up and down along the slippery seam of my sex. I'm so wet. The pulsing friction is hard and all-consuming.

He surges even faster and is slickly sliding along just the right spot. I'm already on sensory overload. My muscles are quivering, my whole body begging for release. His pressure moves a micron to the right, and I'm catapulted over the top. I explode into an amazing orgasm, biting his furred shoulder to keep from screaming out loud for all the others to hear.

My inner muscles still pulsing in aftershocks of pleasure, I relax as I descend from that earth-shattering full-body orgasm. I'm weak, satiated. It's too much work to lift the corners of my mouth in the smile I want to flash at him. My gaze connects and holds his, even as I wonder how I had such mind-blowing pleasure without penetration.

"Wow."

He smiles at me. The first time I've seen him do it. Holy shit, that is a wonderful sight! The tension he always carries has disappeared. He's fully in this moment and there is absolutely no doubt he is digging me and I am digging him back.

For the first time, I see those long, potentially deadly fangs in all their glory. Instead of being scary, I'm simply struck by our differences. I gaze at my pale fingers pressed into the warm, golden fur on his shoulders. If I was an artist, I would paint this. The contrast is beautiful. And sexy.

Even though I just had a Grade A, Defcon 1, over-the-top orgasm, I'm ready for more. His granite-hard cock is still lying along my cleft. He's moving up and down in micro-pulses and I'm ramped up again in just a few moments.

His small strokes become longer and harder. I completely lose my mind and now all I can do is whisper one word, over and over. "Please, please, please." I don't even know what I'm begging for. I want it all. I want everything he can give me.

"Yes, Anya," he promises. He stops for the tiniest moment and shares a look with me. Reaching into the depths of my eyes and my soul, I think, to make certain this is consensual. Hell yes!

He lines himself up with my entrance—both of us are already bathed in my juices, and in one firm, deep plunge he seats himself fully inside me. I focus on the incredible feeling of fullness as he presses into me. We're two perfect pieces of a puzzle.

As I'm still adjusting to the wonderful feeling of being stretched, he thrusts in a delicious rhythm.

I'm enthralled, in a haze of physical bliss. I can't think in words, I can only focus on this pleasure. His rhythm changes—faster. Now punctuating every thrust with an extra little circular motion with his pelvis that has my sensitive nub in ecstasy. My hands are on his butt cheeks, urging him on. He's breathing in my ear, whispering my name.

"Come for me, Anya," he commands quietly.

And I do. My inner muscles clench him in delicious spasms of ecstasy. I bite his shoulder again, trying to be quiet when what I really want to do is scream his name so loud they can hear me back on Earth. Every muscle in my body tightens and then relaxes in blissful release as my orgasm roars through me.

I'm still contracting around his cock when he reaches his own release. The muscles under my palms tighten as he ejaculates into me deeply, then he relaxes.

Without withdrawing from my body, he flips us over, with me sprawled on top of him.

Amazingly, we're still under the blanket. He looks so peaceful, so handsome, as he holds my gaze.

We are just allowed that small moment of afterglow when the PA system interrupts with the orders to complete the act. We hear all the other couples stir and begin to do their business while Zar pets my face and I sneak kisses to his palm.

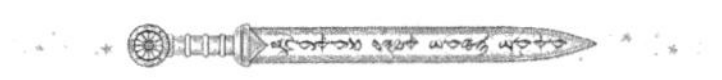

ZAR

I am an idiot.

I punch the heavy bag in the small weight room off the main area of the *ludus*. Luckily, I'm alone in here and not with one of my comrades. I don't want to have to explain my rage, or my misery. I simply want to attack this innocent swinging bag.

I am a fool.

I stop punching and just shake my head in disgust—at myself. I've had no formal education, not like Pallatin. But I've always known I was smart in other ways. Living as a slave my entire life has taught me to be cunning and given me a healthy dose of self-preservation.

One thing I do not need—I slam my fists into the bag in rapid succession—is to feel emotion toward another living being.

I do not need the distraction. Slam.

I definitely do not need the hope. Slam, slam, slam.

I do not need to believe I will ever be anything other than a slave. Slam.

Having hope is a luxury I can't afford. Slam.

And believing that I have fallen in love with Anya? Slam.

That is absolute insanity!

I look down and notice my knuckles are bleeding. By the look of it, they've been bleeding for a while.

I circle the small room. First at a walk, then a run. The movement doesn't give me any relief, yet I can't bear to stand still.

I feel so helpless. I try to get a handle on these emotions, but they are completely out of my control. My stomach heaves. For a moment I feel the urge to vomit, but that passes after I squat and lower my head between my knees, grabbing gulps of air.

I know I shouldn't care about Anya. I shouldn't believe for even half a *minima* that we could overthrow our taskmasters. Hope is for gullible fools. In a few days, we'll arrive on Hyperion and be sold at auction. Anya and I will wind up on different planets. We'll never see each other again. This isn't just foolish, caring about her is dangerous. For me.

But I do care about Anya. And Gods help me if I go forward with this... this what? This relationship? Is that what it is? It's *not* a relationship. It's two people thrown into a cell and forced to mate. That she's not forcing me to do anything makes her attractive to me.

I don't hate her the way I've hated the others. But lack of hate does not make this anything more than what it is—a desperate attempt to connect with the second living being who has never tried to hurt me. But she will. If I allow this to go any farther, when our masters separate us, it will feel almost as bad as when I lost Pallatin.

I make a pact with myself. I can enjoy sex with Anya. I'm a grown male with a fully functioning body. It's healthy to enjoy the sex. Besides, we have to do it anyway. But whatever I think I'm feeling for her? That's got to stop. What we do in bed? That is just mechanics. My heart? I don't have one. I let my walls down for a moment. But now they're back up and battened down tight.

Chapter Six

Anya

This morning, upon my return from medbay, I summon Tyree in my thoughts and she hears me. This proves another leap in her abilities.

The first thing she excitedly tells me is that she got the captain to put his boots on the wrong feet. He wore them for about an hour before he realized.

It means I have some power over him! She explained with excitement. *I have to practice more before I can make him turn off the collars, but I'm getting stronger.*

We have a long talk and in less than an hour, I've collected a ton of information. Like how many crew there are: captain, first mate, doctor, four Urluts, two mechanics, and two low-level humanoid grunts who do everything from cook to clean to laundry. That's eleven of them versus ten gladiators. The captain, first mate, and mechanics may have some military training and fighting experience, but from what Tyree tells me, the two helpers will put up about as much fight as the doctor, and I don't think the doc ever threw a punch in his life.

Even though our side will be completely out-gunned, I think we have a fighting chance! And frankly, I don't believe I'll survive if we don't engage in this battle. I think of Zar's dead eyes and I know I don't want to become like that. I nod my head as I decide that win or lose, I'm all in for this confrontation. If it's to the death, so be it.

I pace my small cell, realizing I don't know if I'll be alive in a week. There is a chance I might be pregnant with a Ton'arr/human baby. I don't know if we'll have this insurrection. Or if we'll win or lose. And if we win? Can I ever return to Earth? I'm certainly not going back if I'm pregnant. Hell, Earth hasn't evolved enough to tolerate other skin colors and religions. Humans aren't ready to accept lion people from outer space.

I'm shocked as I realize I've morphed from the woman who stood in the grocery store freezer section debating which Lean Cuisine to buy, to masterminding an insurrection. I don't know how I changed so quickly. Desperation, maybe. I fully accepted the situation I'm in, realized no one is coming to save me, and am figuring out how to make my life better. I've accepted that I'm here on a spaceship a million miles from home—never to return. Never to return? Wow, that concept is too big to ponder right now.

I cup my hands and grab a drink of water from the sink. When I realize I'm still a bundle of nerves, I shake my head as if I could fling all my worry thoughts out of my mind.

When Zar returns to our cell, I know something's wrong before the barred door clangs shut behind him. He barely makes eye contact, then heads to the sink to wash up. Does he think I can't tell he just took a shower in the *ludus* as he does every day? His hair's still damp. I'm not an idiot. He's "washing up" so he can turn his back to me and not look me in the eye. I'm having none of this!

"Are you ashamed?" I stand up and approach him, hands on hips. "Are you so ashamed of what we did this morning that you can't look me in the eye?"

He doesn't turn, doesn't respond.

"It was a mistake." His voice is soft. He's still facing the back wall.

"Fuck you, Zar! Fuck you very much!" My nostrils flare. My eyes would throw flames if they could.

He delays a full minute or two, waiting, I guess, for me to carry the conversation. I won't do that. This is on him.

"Neither of us can afford to develop feelings for each other. You said yourself we'll be on Hyperion in less than a week." His shoulders slump.

Here we are in the middle of this heavy conversation and a portion of my brain is ridiculously focused on the movement of dozens of perfectly formed muscles shifting under the golden fur on his back. What I should do is focus on the total rejection he is dishing at me right now.

"They are going to sell us off to the highest bidder. We'll be separated from each other within *hoaras* of touchdown." He finally turns to look at me. "Every moment I spend getting closer to you will just kill me a little more when they take you away from me."

His face is a mask of misery.

I walk to him, place my palms softly on his chest, and feel the steady thrum of his heart. I could fall into those golden feline eyes and just live there forever. I stand on tiptoes and whisper in his ear, "We are going to fight them, Zar. We may win or we may die, but we are *not* being sold or separated on Hyperion."

He stands perfectly still for what seems like minutes. His face gives nothing away, but I have a feeling his mind is running like a computer—calculating odds, comparing and contrasting alternate scenarios, and maybe, just maybe, consulting his heart.

He heaves a heavy sigh. "You are willing to die?" His brow lowers with the question.

"Yes." I nod, totally serious.

"I am willing to die, Anya. But you..." He adamantly shakes his mahogany-maned head as his tail lashes. "That I will not allow. I will fight. I will convince my brother gladiators to fight. I will tear the Urluts apart with fangs and claws without any weapons at all if I must. I will do everything in my power to make this happen. But I will *not* participate unless you are safely in this cell." He stubbornly points to the floor.

Whoa, I've never seen this look on his face before. It is fearsome! His handsome jaw is set. It's clear he will brook no argument.

"That's not fair, Zar. It's *my* plan. I can't ask you to risk your life while I'm eating bonbons in a safe room."

"This is non-negotiable." He folds his arms across his chest. "Non-negotiable."

I rub my face, then pace—no small feat in such a tiny space. I never intended to sit back and watch as everyone but me risked their lives. Until a few days ago, I worked in a call center for fuck's sake! The bravest thing I'd ever done was fly down a zip line strapped with twenty pounds of safety rigging.

I don't know who this Anya is, but I know she was born about twenty minutes after she woke up on this ship. And frankly, I *like* her. I don't relish the idea of sitting this one out while the males risk their lives.

On the other hand, I don't know how to fight. I don't know how to shoot a gun, much less an alien version of one. Not to mention I'm slightly klutzy and not very strong. As I envision how all of this would go down, I can't see myself as being a big asset to the team other than as an unqualified, not to mention ungainly, cheerleader.

I'm not totally useless, I remind myself. I have masterminded a lot of this. Tyree has contributed a lot, and Zar has helped me run scenarios and strategize. But it's mostly me who's pulling all of this together. Maybe figuring this out and organizing it and yeah, maybe cheering everyone on *is* the best use of my talents. Besides, the timing of this has to be when the men are in the *ludus*, and I would be locked in here, anyway.

"You're right, dammit," I grudgingly admit.

"Good, we won't argue about this again," he proclaims, as if it is an edict from a king.

"You were ready to bail on us about ten minutes ago, weren't you?"

"Bail?"

"Stop us from being a team?"

"I stand before you a strong warrior. I have faced things in battle you probably couldn't imagine." He takes a deep, heavy breath. "But losing you, Anya... losing you would kill me."

My heart slams in my chest. Zar just admitted his deep feelings for me. I'm not sure what to do with this information, but it makes me inordinately happy. I can't wait for lights out when I can attack him.

Chapter Seven

The next day, I'm sparring in the *ludus* when Captain Gren's voice booms over the loudspeaker.

"We are being pursued by a Marauder pirate vessel," his voice is tense and pressured. "They've come up on us fast and are ready for battle. Marauders are insane and bloodthirsty. They'll fight to the death and take no prisoners."

I've heard tales of the Marauders for many *annums*. Some of the badly scarred males who came to the *ludus* whispered of run-ins with these outlaws. Every time someone talks about them, the versions of their origins are different.

The story that makes the most sense is that somehow the inmates of Matrica II, the infamous prison planet, overthrew their guards and stole a docked freighter. The band of crazed psychopaths evidently grew, overthrew other prison planets, and now there are dozens, possibly hundreds, of ships haphazardly roaming the galaxy in search of small vessels to attack. They board, kill and rape passengers and crew, then commandeer the ships.

From the tales I've heard, the lucky ones are killed, then raped and not the other way around. I wonder if the whispers about cannibalism are true. Anya and the other females have no way of knowing any of this. If we're overpowered, they will be completely vulnerable—awaiting a terrible fate.

The ship heaves, clearly taking evasive maneuvers at high speed. Before I can think of my own safety, my thoughts veer to Anya. How can I possibly protect her?

One of the three Urluts guarding us rushes out of the *ludus*, I presume toward the bridge. The remaining guards are on high alert, watching all ten of us.

"Each of you face the wall. On your knees! Leave ten *fiertos* between you. Hands on the back of your heads," Lurco orders. "We will kill anyone who makes a move."

In this position, it's hard not to fall every time the ship swerves sharply. I try to keep my center of gravity low. If I tip to the side, a trigger-happy guard will blast my head off.

I'm sure every other male here is worried about the Marauder attack and saving their own lives. I'm more worried about Anya than myself.

The ship veers sharply, then there's the wrenching sound of metal tearing. As if there was any doubt, the captain's clipped voice announces, "We've been hit. The hull's been breached. I see dozens of Marauder heat signatures invading through the opening."

"You've got to let us loose," I shout over many voices exclaiming at once. "We're trained fighters. Let us protect ourselves." I quickly add, "And you."

"Alright, assholes, you have one chance." Lurco is trying to keep command, but sounds panicked. "Stand up if you're willing to fight."

All of us stand slowly, so they don't get an itch to blast our collars.

"Don't forget, all we have to do is press a button and you're all dead. Your task is to fight against the crazies. If you so much as make a move against one of the ship's staff, we will kill you without asking a question. Got it?"

We all nod our heads, still facing the wall, waiting for his orders.

"Lurco," the captain announces overhead, "give each gladiator a laser weapon from the armory. You men still have activated collars around your necks. You're fighting for your lives here today. If you turn those guns toward any of this ship's crew, we will blow your head off your shoulders. I hope my orders are understood."

"Humberg," the captain adds, "as soon as you've armed the men, bring six of them to the bridge on the double. Lurco, take Helix and the other four slaves to the cell block."

The Marauders are crazy, but they're said to be fighting machines. They've already boarded our vessel and are looking for fresh meat. We are in for a nasty battle. I have no idea how many of them there are. But with ten gladiators, all armed with real weapons, we'll put up a hell of a fight!

As Lurco gives the order to line up and march to the armory, Shadow sidles up to me. "This is the time, Zar!" he whispers. "Now is the time to wage our insurrection." His eye is bright. He looks more alive than I've ever seen him.

"Are you crazy, Shadow? Our collars are active. We'd be waging war against two enemy factions, not only the ship's staff but the Marauders as well. And the females! They would all be killed within *minimas* if we fight our captors now."

"Your female has made you soft. I give absolutely no fucks about the female I share a cell with. Now is the time."

"You've lost yourself, Shadow. You have so much hate in you that you can't think straight. Even if you don't care about anyone on this ship but yourself, your plan will not work. The collars, Shadow. We have to deactivate the collars or we'll all be dead. Today we fight against the Marauders. Soon, soon we will fight the males of this ship."

Shadow's jaw clenches as he seems to be weighing my words. He must see I'm right. He nods his head, almost imperceptibly, then gets in line.

Although I've been raised to fight since my first memory, I've only been trained in the gladiator weapons of old. There are many types of gladiators, each with its own weaponry and shields. My specialty is murmillo. I fight in competition with an elongated shield and a three *fierto* double-edged sword. I've never even touched a weapon designed within the last two thousand *annums*.

Lurco's lesson in using the laser blasters consists of no more than, "Point and shoot." I don't want to be overconfident, but there seems to be no art in this.

Having no idea how many bursts I can fire with one power pack, I don't know if my strategy should be to conserve energy or just blast anything that moves. I think of Anya and know she must be frantic as she waits helplessly in her cell. She's trapped with nowhere to go. If the Marauders come upon her deck before we get to them, she'll be raped or killed immediately.

"You six go with Humberg to the bridge," Lurco orders. "You four, come with Helix and me to the cell block."

My lucky day. I'm on my way to protect Anya.

Anya

Holy shit! Talk about being a sitting duck! Here we are in our cells, open to the world with no protection. Even though the captain said these guys take no prisoners, I don't think I've ever seen a movie like this where the attackers came on board and didn't ravage the women.

Looking for something I can use as a weapon, I inspect my bed and discover the platform is not made of springs. Of course not. That might have afforded a modicum of comfort. Under the thin mattress is one piece of solid metal welded to four sturdy legs.

This might provide some protection when the Marauders storm in. Only one problem, the damn thing is secured to the floor with inch-thick bolts. Can I not catch a break?

There is nothing in the cell but the bed, the thin blanket, the toilet, and a sink. The sink! I remember the sink stopper thingy is removable, then go over to grab it. The top flange looks to be the correct size to use as a makeshift screwdriver. I fly over to the nearest leg of the bed and try my improvised method. Lo and behold, it fits and is unscrewing the bolts.

I scream at the top of my lungs, competing with the blare of the klaxons, "Ladies, unscrew your bed from the floor. Use the sink stopper. You can use your bed as a shield!"

I keep unscrewing as I hear my instructions being repeated down the line. This may just be busywork so we don't freak about being zapped into char by the Marauders' lasers, but it's better than sitting still and biting my nails.

Zar

It takes forever to arrive at the cellblock thanks to these *dracking* Urluts. They're so slow and ungainly we could move faster if we picked them up and carried them over our shoulders. I'm relieved to see the door hasn't been breached. We've heard weapon fire elsewhere in the ship, so we must be arriving here just in time. I step into the corridor only far enough to see my Anya on hands and knees frantically working at releasing the bolts holding the bed to the floor.

"Anya," I call to her and my heart squeezes in my chest when she lifts her head and smiles apprehensively at me. "We'll protect you and the others." Now that I've reassured myself she's safe, I stride back to the only door into the cell block. I hear the enemy approaching down the connecting corridor and can no longer pretend to defer to the Urluts. I simply take over.

"Guards, release the cell doors. Have all the women move to the last cell in the cell block." They don't resist my command, I think they're relieved to be following orders rather than giving them.

"Females, hurry!" I roar over the cacophony of horns and weapon fire.

"Dax, Steele, Stryker! Carry the beds back to them. Make a protective barrier between them and us." The men fall in, quickly grabbing the beds the females have released from the floor, then hustling them to form a makeshift wall for the women to crouch behind. I hear a few grunts as my men pull some partially bolted beds out of the floor with sheer brute strength.

"They're coming," I shout. "Each male stay in a cell. Hide until the Marauders are all past the threshold." I didn't have to order the Urluts to hide. They were already rushing to cower in the first cell. Great news, they can serve as a distraction to the enemy. While the Marauders are busy killing Lurco and Helix in the first cell, we can blast the bastards to hell.

An unknown number of Marauders rush through the doorway. I'm in the second cell with Dax, but I can see their reflections on the metal wall. They look crazy as shit. A few are naked. A few are wearing bizarre layers of clothes and blankets. Even though I'm seeing all of this so quickly and through a distorted reflection, the most striking thing I see is all the red. They all seem covered in red. I don't know if it's blood or paint or both, but they're screaming and laughing and singing—their obvious insanity could terrify an untrained enemy.

They stop whooping and hollering all at once. They've discovered the guards in the first cell. There is a long eerie moment of silence and then the sound of intense laser fire. I stand ready with my weapon.

If I'm not mistaken, I hear laser fire being returned by the Urluts. By the sounds of things, they may have even slain a few of the enemy.

A moment of calm while the Marauders take a moment to reload. As soon as they step into our line of sight, Dax and I fire. "Now!" I yell to the others. I'm too focused on firing my weapon to look down the hallway, but I imagine Steele and Stryker coming out of hiding and firing into the bottleneck of Marauders.

The fighting is intense. The noise of laser fire is thunderous and nonstop. There is a smell so putrid it steals my breath. I have no time to pay attention to anything other than firing my weapon. There are so many of the enemy that even though we've killed perhaps a dozen of them, the rest keep coming. They're just stepping over their own dead, streaming down the hallway, intent upon killing whatever living beings they find.

They're slipping on the blood of their comrades, still whooping and singing as if they're at a party. I could never have imagined behavior like this. There is no organization, no plan, just forward motion and laser fire.

The way the cell block is set up, they don't have a chance. They're easy prey with nowhere to turn, just working their way forward into our line of fire.

Within a *minima*, laser fire stops. I take a moment longer to make sure there isn't another phalanx of them on their way. But this wing of the ship is quiet.

"Ho," Stryker shouts, "all seems clear."

"Females! Stay down," I holler. First, I count the heads of my gladiators. All present and accounted for—good. Then a body count of the pileup near the first cell where all the action was. It looks like twenty-one dead. I see movement near the bottom of the pile and spray the entire mound with enough laser fire to kill a battalion.

When I look into the first cell, I see Lurco's body has been all but obliterated by laser fire. Helix appears badly wounded, but still breathes.

"Anya? Are you okay?"

"Yes?" her voice is shaky, but after jogging to take a look, I see no charred remnants of laser fire on the bedframes the females were hiding behind.

"Dax, come with me. We need to search for any who might be hiding." Having seen the insanity of the Marauders' behavior, it's hard to imagine any of them could lurk quietly in the shadows. They would more likely be singing or screaming somewhere.

"This may not be over. The females need to stay where they are," I say with authority.

We search the hallways, cargo holds, and rooms thoroughly, but it looks like no Marauders survived. We run into three other gladiators when we've almost reached the bridge.

"We killed a dozen," Shadow reports. "We've searched the starboard side for stragglers. The ship's clean."

I heave a sigh of relief and lead my men back to the cell block, my stomach clenched in worry about Anya with every step. When we arrive there, the captain booms over the loudspeaker, "We have subdued all intruders on the bridge. How are things in the cell block?"

Helix presses his comm and weakly relates, "Lurco is gone. I'm wounded. All Marauders are good and dead."

It's only now I grab Dax's arm, pulling him to the back of the cell block so he can help me remove the bed frames and release the women.

It's the work of a moment to heft the bed frames out of the makeshift wall. Although she assured me she was alive, I breathe a sigh of relief when I see Anya's beautiful face. Her pale skin and enormous eyes reveal the toll the last few *hoaras* have taken on her.

After quickly checking to see none of the other women have been injured, my entire concern is on Anya as she hurries to my side and nestles under my arm. She gets so close it's as if she's trying to melt into my body.

"Zar." She puts her palms to my cheeks, then pulls back to inspect me from mane to toes. "You're safe!" She squeezes next to me again, hugging me tight enough to almost steal my breath.

"Aye, Little One. We're both safe."

Chapter Eight

ANYA

We spend the rest of the day cleaning up the mess. At first, my hands are shaking so badly I'm useless. I'm still so unnerved I don't want to be more than two inches from Zar.

My past life as an office worker was boring. I didn't grow up in a family that hunted or collected guns. The closest I've been to anything like this was... never. I can't even think of a time in my history where I was ever in real danger. But after a few minutes at Zar's side, I begin to calm down, and my system eases from high alert to code yellow.

As I move along the cellblock corridor, it's my first interaction with most of these... beings. I've seen most of the men march past me twice a day on their way to and from the *ludus*. I've seen the women on their way to medbay. But now we're allowed to work shoulder to shoulder, and I get some up close and personal time with a few of them.

I've only seen Shadow when I've been marched past his cell in the mornings. He's pretty creepy. He looks very humanoid, but he's one scarred-up mess, with a robotic-prosthetic eye and left arm. No one here is really a happy camper. I mean, we're all slaves, right? But Shadow is like the black hole of anger. Zar mentioned even the gladiators give him a wide berth.

He doesn't pay any attention to his cellmate, Grace. Most of the other couples are working together to get the bunks put back together, but Grace is on her own while Shadow prowls around. What a dick!

All the other guys seem considerate of "their" women, though. I notice the males doing all the heavy lifting. The women seem at ease with their cellies. It looks as though they're faring okay. Good, I've been worrying about their treatment.

The Urluts are down one man, two if you count the guy who got injured. Since that pile of dead Marauders was unceremoniously dragged out of the cell block and dumped, I assume, into the silent depths of outer space, we've been locked in the cell block together with no guards.

I decide it's a good time to quietly conspire now that we're mingling together. I still assume someone might be listening, so I put myself in stealth mode.

"Zar, is there anyone who's not on board with the escape?" I whisper when he's within earshot. "Could I talk to them?"

"Steele is noncommittal. I think he's worried about his female getting harmed in reprisal if our attempt fails."

Gee, that warms my heart. Glad to hear he cares about one of my comrades. Her name is Zoey. She's in the cell adjoining us, on the opposite side of Grace and Shadow. I've tried to strike up a conversation with her a couple of times, but she's super timid. She doesn't talk. That educational video of exploding heads they showed us when we first boarded must have made quite an impression on her.

They're both in their cell. She's crouching in the corner, and he's screwing bolts back into the floor. A tiny woman with nondescript shoulder-length hair, she was kidnapped in jeans and a t-shirt. If I'm not mistaken, she's wearing a bra. Lucky her! She gives me a shy smile when I introduce myself. I don't hold out my hand for a shake, figuring being forced to touch me just might tilt her world off its axis. I want to gain her trust, not scare her.

He's a humanoid guy except his skin is silver. His name certainly fits. He's built like a brick house and is sexy-looking in a dangerous sort of way.

"So," I barge in pretty much without preamble, "we're arriving on Hyperion in a matter of days. I'm told it's a hellhole where the scum of the galaxy gathers to do dirty deals."

I whisper matter-of-factly, "My understanding is that we women will probably be sold off to the highest bidder. We'll probably fetch a higher price if we're already pregnant with a gladiator's baby. They're going to sell the guys as well. I don't see any reason we'd be sold off as pairs." I figure if these two have bonded, this might be a motivator for them to want to join the revolution.

"I think we've figured out a way to turn off the collars," I pointedly look at Zoey, who's been fingering her collar since I entered their cell. "I had figured our chances to liberate ourselves were good *before* one of the Urluts was killed and another seriously injured. Now I think our chances are even better."

Steele still appears skeptical, and Zoey looks at him expectantly, waiting for him to make the decision.

"Steele, I think everyone else is on board with the plan. If nine out of ten gladiators are revolting, our owners aren't going to give a shit if you're in or out. You're a slave—they're going to kill everyone in the uprising. They're not going to spare you because you didn't participate. I think you'd protect Zoey better if you fought with us than if you were hanging back trying to keep out of it."

I have his full attention at this point. He has an intelligent look about him. I assume he's weighing all the odds while he doesn't take his eyes off Zoey for a second. Aww, that is so cute. I think he likes her—so protective.

"Where will the females be when we attack?" His look is so serious I imagine he's running scenarios in the back of his head even as he's listening to me.

"The attack will be when you're training. Usually, they leave us in this cell block alone during that time. Being two guards down, I think it's a safe bet we'll be unattended. You guys will make your move and hopefully kill your two guards, get their six weapons, and be on your way to the bridge before anyone knows there's a problem."

He wipes his palm across his mouth, deep in thought.

"At that point, the folks on the bridge will be preoccupied with saving their own asses from a marauding band of angry gladiators. The last thing they're going to throw resources at is even thinking about the women locked in their cells.

"Worry about yourself, Steele. Taking over this ship will be a true battle. I think we women will only be an afterthought."

He nods thoughtfully, then eases over to Zoey. He slowly crouches, then leans in to talk to her, as if she's a shy baby doe he's afraid will bolt. He whispers. She listens and then nods cautiously.

"I'm in."

I start to thank him, but he interrupts.

"One condition."

I wait, having no idea what he's going to ask.

"Zoey's... fearful. I worry about her when I'm not here. Will you talk to her when I'm in the *ludus*? Will you take care of her when things go down?"

"Absolutely, Steele. Absolutely."

"Okay then, we're in."

A moment later, I'm telling Zar those two are on board. He beams at me with pride. Him gazing at me that way feels almost as good as when he looks at me like he wants to eat me up—and I mean that in a good way.

Zar's busy mopping up gallons—and I do mean gallons—of blood that are coagulating near the door exiting the cell block. The Marauder contingent was truly a ragtag bunch of males and females. When I took a peek at that pile, I saw at least ten different species of aliens. I saw blue, red, green, and gold skin in all shapes and sizes. This was the craziest scum of the entire galaxy squeezed into one pirate ship.

Somebody's blood smells like moldy cheese on steroids, and I think all of us are working hard to stifle our gag reflexes. The quicker this gets poured down the toilets, the better we'll all breathe. Thank God Zar is not asking me to help. I have my limits, and I think I've just reached them.

"Anybody else I should talk to?" I ask, now more confident than ever.

"I haven't been able to catch Axxios. For some reason, we're never alone with each other for even a moment." He covers his mouth and nose with both hands, trying to get a breath of non-contaminated air. The wretched look on his face when he gets back to mopping tells me he wasn't successful.

"Axxios?" Sorry, it's hard to keep them all straight.

"He's...." He leans his mop against his chest and encircles his neck, fingers three inches away from his fur. "Big. And gold."

"Got it, thanks." I wander back down the hallway. Shouldn't be hard to find Axxios.

He's a big man, and yes, his neck is... well, he has no neck. His muscles just go from shoulder to head. He's a gorgeous shade of luminous gold.

"Axxios?"

He looks up, politely nods at me, then bows. Sooo not what I expected.

"You are Zar's mate?"

Well, I never thought of it that way, but, "Yes. I guess I am."

Axxios continues with formal introductions as he courteously motions for his cellmate to join us. "May I introduce Brianna?" She smiles cordially. "Brianna this is…?"

"Oh, sorry." I hold out my hand, "Anya. Zar's… mate."

"Zar is?"

"The lion guy," I offer. "Down there," I point to him, now mostly covered in stinky alien blood at the end of the hall. They wave at each other cordially. Could this get more surreal?

I give Brianna a quick once-over. She's a BBW, cute in a quiet, unassuming librarian kind of way. How she manages to look positively prim in that flimsy nightgown escapes me.

I figure I'll just launch into it before they offer me tea and crumpets. I lean close and whisper, "We're planning a revolt." Oh, this is a hard audience. Poker faces, both of them.

I explain about Hyperion, being sold when we get there, that we might have a way to turn the collars off, and all I receive are dispassionate stares. Are these two alive or are they wax figures?

"May I ask who is going to pilot this ship after we… dispose of the captain?" Axxios inquires good-naturedly.

"We can't kill the captain. We're going to have to collar him and watch him 24/7." 24/7? He won't know what that means. Like a hawk? No. "We'll have to watch him constantly," I amend.

"Would you be amenable to me flying the craft?"

What? Either he's delusional or we just stepped into the best piece of luck in the history of the universe.

"Excuse me? Did you just imply you know how to pilot one of these things?"

"Well, I haven't captained a ship this small for many *annums*, but yes, I'm authorized to fly a ship of this class. I was in the group that was on the bridge today. After we dispatched the Marauders, I got a good look around. I can absolutely fly this craft."

I want to yell "holy shit," do a victory dance, and high five handsome no-neck guy, but I think he might look at me like I'm a turd in the punchbowl, so I say only, "You, sir, have made my day."

"Yes indeed, what could be better than being attacked and almost killed by a troop of Marauders?" he asks with a deliciously wry sense of humor.

"I think I like you, Axxios. So can I count you two in?"

The two huddle together, well, not too close of a huddle, wouldn't want to touch each other in front of strangers, would they? It doesn't take long before they give each other the smallest of smiles and in unison tell me, "We're in!"

I've already taken a few steps down the hall, but turn on my heel and head back. "Axxios, those Marauders breached our hull. How is it we haven't been sucked into space?"

He looks at me tolerantly, like an adult just asked him how to spell "dog."

"I assume fixing the breach was the first order of business. First, the captain would use judicious hatch closures to isolate the damage. Most ships carry extra materials, self-healing metal panels applied by competent mechanics probably did the trick."

"Okay, thanks." Maybe I've seen one too many sci-fi movies. I have a lot to worry about, but being sucked into the quiet vacuum of space isn't one of them.

Chapter Nine

Zar

Perhaps our owners took pity on us. First, the males and then the females were allowed into the *ludus* to shower. None of us smelled very fresh, but because of all that blood from the Marauders clinging to my fur, I was the worst. My tail dragged through a river of it, even though I'd tried to keep it in the air.

Another bonus is that we got some kind of rations other than the ubiquitous bars Anya says taste like glue and sawdust. I'm not sure what they served us was much better than our usual fare. It was tinned meat and starch of some kind, possibly rations hidden in storage in case we were stranded in space. I overheard a couple of the women in the cell block begging for bars after opening their cans.

Anya sniffed hers, delicately dipped the tip of her tongue in it, pronounced, "Tastes like Joyous Jane Chicken and Dumplings," and dug in. I followed suit. I'm not sure what Joyous Jane Chicken and Dumplings are, but I will guarantee little Anya enjoyed it far more than I did.

The tins are now rinsed and placed outside our cell. We're sitting on the bed, and Anya is swinging her legs. I'm content just watching her.

She reaches out and runs her fingers through my mane. I'm always surprised at her little moments of genuine affection, and even more surprised at how deeply they please me.

"I worried about you today." She looks into my eyes, her palm on my cheek.

"I had to force myself not to worry about you. My distraction could have endangered both of us." I pause a moment, then admit, "But half my thoughts were on you the entire battle."

She falls silent, just grinning at me. My body is aching from the unaccustomed activity and high alert I've been on, but all I can do is think about the delights I hope await me after lights out.

"So, I was waiting to tell you the best news ever." She kind of sings the last few words of this sentence in excitement. She waits for my response.

"Are you going to make me beg?"

"I found us a pilot!"

"In a hidden room?" I jest.

"Funny." She playfully punches my shoulder. "Axxios is a pilot, big boy."

"A pilot of what? How do you know he can fly this ship?"

"Well, I didn't ask for a copy of his resume, but he seemed like a straight shooter and intimated he was used to far bigger craft than this."

"What are the odds of this?" My brow furrows in thought.

"You don't believe me? Don't believe him? What?"

I'm silent for a moment, not sure how to tell her. Wondering if she'll think less of me, but I decide to tell her anyway.

"I haven't told you a lot about my childhood. I think you know some basics. Raised by uncaring caregivers, sold at my owners' whims when they were angry, down on their luck, or maybe just wanted to buy racing stock instead of fighting stock.

"Most of my education came from fellow fighters, and they hailed from around the galaxy with a wide range of religious beliefs. I've listened to a few males who spoke of their God or Gods in glowing tones and tried to convert me. I've learned about other beliefs during some of their holy days. My head is full of a jumble of ideas about God, and I'm not sure what I believe.

"But that out of twenty souls, twenty souls in our tiny insurrection and one of them is equipped to fly this vessel, more than equipped if what you say is correct, doesn't that say something? Doesn't that say perhaps we are blessed?"

I grasp her hand between my palms.

"Blessed by who, blessed by what, I have no idea. But certainly, fate has smiled on us, Anya."

I pause for a moment and look deeply into those beautiful green eyes of hers. "Anya, you winding up in this cell, with me... you've saved my life. No matter what happens when we rise up against them, win or lose, know this—you've saved my life."

A stroke of luck and the lights flick off at the end of my declaration. I probably shouldn't have blurted that out. Perhaps it was too much to dump on her. She hasn't said a word.

Her weight lifts off the mattress and I hear the soft sounds of her clothes being shed. She kneels at my feet and presses my knees apart, nestling between my thighs.

Her hands are gentle as she tries to remove my loincloth. I take pity on her. It's a complicated series of twists and knots. While I'm busy with that, she strokes my inner thighs. All but one of the dim lights that illuminate the cell block at night were shot out in the laser fire. We are nearly bathed in darkness. I can't fully see her face, her hands, or her expressions. I can only feel.

I never knew my thighs were capable of such sensual feelings, but my attention is fully focused on the whisper-soft tracing of her fingers and then her palms stroking my fur from knees to the crease of my torso. My cock has been hard since I felt her kneeling at my feet, but now it's straining in her direction.

Kisses. Slow kisses from inner knee up my thigh in a lazy zigzag, as if there is all the time in the world. One leg, then the other. I have no thoughts other than what is happening in this moment.

Dear Gods, she is nipping me. Her blunt teeth gently scraping me, knee to thigh and back again. Now her tongue is tracing delicate patterns through my fur, touching sensitive skin underneath. She's spending an exorbitant amount of time in the crease between thigh and torso. Every cell in my body is on high alert. She bends forward and tongues the area above my cock, on my belly.

I don't know how she is doing it, but she manages to avoid my jutting cock, which is straining toward her, demanding to be touched.

"Not yet," she says firmly, and then breathes onto my skin, licking and nipping. Meanwhile, her hands have pushed me back full length onto the bed, so she has perfect access to me. I gently pull her mouth toward my cock, letting her know it's time to get down to business, but she pushes my hands away and orders, "Lie back. You're not allowed to touch me, just feel."

Oh, I'm feeling alright. I'm feeling I will explode if this keeps up much longer. But little Anya is clearly in no hurry as she works her way around, this way and that, everywhere but where I am dying for her to be. A sense of urgency builds, spiking through me. Even my blood is running hot.

And finally, her warm breath is on the head of my cock. Cool breath in, warm breath out. Then it feels even cooler and even warmer, her mouth now open and a micron away from finally touching me.

"Anya," I demand and plead at the same time. I want to order her to touch me, but I don't, realizing how delicious the anticipation is.

Her tongue circles the tip of my cock. I make a deep, rumbling sound in the back of my throat at the same time she whispers, "You taste so good." Clenching my jaw, I try to control the lust sizzling along my veins at the thought she likes my taste.

Her accomplished little tongue dances around and around my tip, then circles the ridge of my crown. When she decides I'm in enough of a wild frenzy, her mouth surrounds my cockhead. I know she likes to keep these things private, but I don't think my growl is subtle at all.

Now there's suction. Up and down, just the head. Up and down and a swirl. Up and down and a swirl. I lose my mind. My hips buck up toward her, wanting to feel this, yes this, on my shaft.

And then I do. Her mouth plunges toward the base in one swift movement—sucking, her tongue twirling, and head bobbing up and down. Such a very gifted tongue. I keep my hands on the bed. I don't want to press her or force her or push her head. But I can't keep my hands still. My fingers and palms roam her shoulders, upper arms and back even as I try not to jam my cock into that talented mouth.

My hand slides to cup her breast, but she elbows my hand away. It's clear she wants her moment of command. Yes, she's in perfect control and I have lost it. My hips are thrusting and every thought has zeroed in on her mouth. Her mouth and my cock.

Finally, perhaps taking pity on me, she climbs onto the bed, straddles me, leans over, and kisses me on the lips. In one movement, she impales herself on my cock. How I manage not to moan in ecstasy, I'll never know. She rides me for a moment, and all patience is gone.

In one swift action, I roll us over, still fully seated inside her warm channel. With one hand, I grab her wrists and hold them above her head. "Now I'm in charge, little Anya." I kiss her lips, her face, her cheeks as I ride her hard, giving no mercy just as she gave me none. My thrusts are forceful and desperate, but she keeps up with me, rising to meet each one.

At the bottom of every thrust, I give that little circular motion I know will push her over the edge. Only a few of these and she slips her hands from my grasp and puts them over her mouth, stifling the scream of pleasure signaling her release.

The exquisite contractions massaging me inside her wet, welcoming channel push me over the edge. Still panting as I come down from that magnificent explosion, I press my back against the wall, turning her on her side so we can stay connected, face to face.

Coupling in the past was always forced, filling me with shame and rage. This feeling is new. No one has ever focused on giving me pleasure. I'm suffused with liquid warmth. A calm I never dreamed of spreads through me. And then my heart squeezes as I'm filled with terror that this amazing, unexpected bliss I've found with Anya will be snatched away on Hyperion.

Anya

I lie facing Zar, taking stock of the situation. I'm a kidnapped breeder in an 8x8 foot cell in a spaceship far from home, family, and friends. I'm planning a dangerous overthrow of aliens with laser guns and exploding shock collars. What's the most surprising part of the equation? This amazing connection I've found with Zar.

I really like this guy and I'm pretty sure he really likes me. I don't think this is Stockholm syndrome. If it was, I'd be attracted to an Urlut, not Zar. I think I read somewhere that people who are in dangerous situations together are way more likely to fall for each other. Whatever... I don't care. Zar is handsome, protective, and makes love like a god. My life would be complete shit without him. I don't see a downside to caring for him.

There are so many question marks in my life right now. Even if our little revolution works perfectly—and the odds are dismal—I have no idea what will happen after that. I don't have any idea who the authorities might be, or what kind of trouble we'll be in. Is this ship within the law? Is it legal to kidnap people? Buy and sell them? If the owners of this ship—the owners of us slaves—are within the law, then *we* will certainly be outside it if we steal this ship.

If the vessel is owned by pirates or smugglers, no authorities will be looking for us. I relax a moment, then my muscles tighten when I replay every movie I've ever seen about someone enraging the mafia. If we're "stealing" from an illegal organization, they are eventually going to want their property back. My stomach clenches in fear.

And then I place my palm on my belly. There's the little issue of a possible lion baby. I don't even want to think about that.

My head is spinning with questions for which I have no answers. My family didn't call me "worrywart" for nothing.

"You're restless, Little One. Why?" Zar asks, his arm a comfortable weight across my middle, his tail wrapped reassuringly around my ankle.

"Just thinking..." I answer evasively.

"Tell me."

"Just worrying about what happens when we take over the ship."

"What about it?"

"Everything." I let it all come spilling out. "Where will we go? How will we find the money to pay for things? How will we evade whoever is going to come after us?"

He chuckles quietly. "Don't you think we should first worry about taking over the ship?"

"It's like a game of chess, a strategy game we have on Earth. In order to win, you have to think many moves ahead."

"You're so smart, my Little Anya. You're right. But tonight, try to get some sleep."

"Can't."

"Tell me about your childhood, your family, your world."

I'm not sure if he really wants to know, or if he's just trying to distract my racing thoughts.

"What do you want to know?"

"Everything. I want to know everything that made you into who you are." His thumb strokes the back of my neck in figure eights.

First, I tell him about the planet. How beautiful it is, how diverse the species are that inhabit it. I neglect to tell him about climate change, greed, and political corruption. I'm not sure I want him to know the trouble my planet is facing.

I talk about the change of seasons—he seems extra fascinated by stories of snow, snowmen, sledding, and the cold. He's never been to a place that had a real winter. I describe a bit about our social structure, and make sure to mention that slavery has been outlawed for centuries.

But it's when I talk about my family that his interest comes alive. He peppers me with questions about the most mundane things. The nuclear family is almost incomprehensible to him.

"So, the two people who make the baby live together? Forever?" He seems gobsmacked by this idea.

"Yes. Not everyone, of course. There are single-parent families..." I don't want to confuse him too much. "The parents often decide to join together in a ceremony, either through the government or through their religion, and then they live together. And they raise the child together."

He nods his head as if this is a difficult concept he's having trouble fully absorbing.

"Tell me more about your parents. How did they treat you?"

The more I tell him, the more questions he asks. "We should probably get to sleep, Zar. Before too long, we're going to hear the order to complete the act."

"One final question," he demands.

"Okay."

"Tell me your favorite story about your father."

I have no idea why that is uppermost on his mind, but I'll comply. I search through my memories and then get a little misty-eyed as I realize how much I miss my parents. If I'm pregnant, even if we take over the ship, I'm not sure I can return to Earth. It might not be an option. I hold back hot tears, then take a breath and continue.

"I was about ten and we went on a camping trip. That's when you leave the comforts of your home and sleep outdoors. Don't ask... it really is as dumb as it sounds. At any rate, we took Freckles the family dog—which is an animal that is a pet."

I can feel him cocking his head in question, so I answer it before he can ask it. "They are living beings, animals, but not humanoid, not sentient. We keep them around to pet them."

"You pet a pet? Did that translate correctly?"

"You keep them around to stroke them, feed them, and take care of them. So, my pet dog, not so smart, ran off the day we had to get back to our home. We looked for him and called him for hours and then had to leave without him. At any rate, I was crazed over it. I cried for days. Freckles and I were a pair. I was bereft."

He leans closer and kisses the top of my head to comfort me. Such a small act. So full of affection.

"So, on my dad's next day off, he put me in the car, and we drove all the way to the campsite. It was hours away. We called the dog for long minutes. My father confessed later that he never believed, not for a second, that the dog would still be in the area. He totally believed that predators would have eaten the dog. But finally, Freckles came limping up. He looked way skinnier, but he was alive and really happy to see us.

"Now that I'm an adult, I realize there was absolutely no reason to believe the dog would be alive. It must have been so hard for Dad to throw away a whole precious day off on a fool's errand. But he did it for me, and I love him a lot for that."

Zar is so quiet I wonder if he's fallen asleep, but his hand is still caressing the back of my neck. Then he meaningfully moves his hand to my belly. "I wish to be that kind of father," he pronounces. "I wish to be the kind of father my youngling can tell loving stories about. I never had a father. I've never actually seen a father, not one in action.

"What if there is a youngling growing in your belly, Anya? What if I've made you pregnant and we do win our rebellion, and I get to be a father and I'm not good at it?" There is sheer panic in his gravelly voice.

The sincerity of his concern wrenches my gut. "My dad wasn't perfect, Zar, but he loved me. Do you think you will love the... youngling when he or she is born? If you do, you'll be a good father."

"A few days ago, I would have told you I can't love. I would have told you I was a stone, incapable of loving anyone or anything. But today," he pauses to make sure I hear these next words, "today I know I'm capable of love. I love you, and I will love the youngling we will make together."

Zar just said he loves me, without preamble or pretense. Part of me wants to tell him I love him back. Part of me is scared to death. I feel shaky. Love is a big word. I don't want to use it until I'm sure. And what if we escape? If we take over this ship, do I want to go back to Earth and never see him again?

I hate to leave him hanging, but I can't say the words yet. I nestle against him and pull his arm around my waist. His tail wraps around my ankle. He does it so often I'm beginning to feel naked without it.

Chapter Ten

Anya

When the announcement wakes us the next morning, I can tell we stayed up way too late last night. I'm still tired, and even Zar, usually so full of energy, seems to move a bit slower than usual.

Our enforced bed session takes longer than when Zar was still "Minute Man." The lights are on. It is not a passionate affair by any means, but we do it face to face while looking deeply into each other's eyes. It feels sexual and intimate, and it deepens our growing connection.

I kiss Zar before the Urluts get to our cell. We both know without discussing it that it's not safe for the Urluts to know Zar and I have feelings for each other. I assume whatever they know can and will be used against us, so we're not openly showing affection in front of them. Who knows if they're watching or recording us? It's too much to worry about.

As Zar passes me to walk to the back of the cell to kneel, hands on top of his head, he winks at me and gives me that sexy, killer smile. OMG, his face lifted in happiness could claim even a dead woman's heart.

Today is the day, I decide. Today I find out more about the doctor. Knowing if he's in our corner is going to be important when we rise up. If he's not on our side, I hate to think about it, but he will have to go on the "to do" list. And not in a good way. I hope we don't have to kill him. I actually like the guy, but overtaking the ship is our top priority.

"Patient C! Still not going to tell me your name?"

He's nothing if not always cheery and upbeat, speculum in hand.

"I'll tell you mine if you tell me yours," I reply, equally congenial.

"Well," he says, patting the exam table with his free hand. "I've been remiss in my duties. I'm Dr. Drayke sun Omron." He bows. "And you?"

"Anya Nash." I do the most awkward curtsy this side of Orion's belt.

"You seem to be in one fine mood this morning, Miss Anya. To what do I owe this pleasure?"

Well, I'm certainly not going to cop to the fact that I'm currently falling for, and getting well fucked by, my gladiator lion guy. "After yesterday's near-death experience with the Marauders, I'm just glad to be alive."

He's surprised, and if I can read him correctly, perhaps a bit guilty. He knows I'm about to be sold into slavery, possibly pregnant with a child I didn't agree to conceive, and then will be separated from it. I damn well hope he's feeling huge gobs of guilt.

"What do I call you?"

"Dr. Drayke is fine, Miss Anya."

I still haven't compliantly hopped up onto the exam table. "I'm assuming that wherever we're headed isn't going to be a bed of roses... a happy place." I spear him with a piercing look. "Can you tell me why they kidnapped us?" I think I know, but I want to hear it from him.

"Human females are considered excellent breeders. They conceive easily, and their DNA mixes well with many other species. Offspring tend to resemble the males." At least he has the decency to look sheepish.

I nod. "That's pretty much what I thought." I try to suppress the anger coiling in my belly. Kidnapped and taken far from home to incubate someone's baby—this is so fucked up. I distract myself by asking, "Do you know what's in store for us?"

He almost pats the table, but I think he knows that ploy will never work. "Anya," he sighs heavily, "you have to know I have no power on board this ship. I'm half a step above janitor. They don't consider me a full-fledged member of the team. They know," he pauses, "they know I was tricked into signing my contract and don't approve of what they're doing. If they didn't need me so badly, I think they'd throw me in the brig along with all of you. I only overhear bits and pieces of their plans at dinner when they don't think I'm listening.

"I'm not sure you want to know what's in store for you. Wouldn't you like to keep your happy mood, even if it's only for a few more days?"

"No, Dr. Drayke, I don't. I'm a realist. I want to know what I'm going to be up against." I think I have a pretty good idea what level of hell awaits us all on Hyperion. But a part of me wonders if he might have some additional information. Another part of me wants to push him to say it.

He stands still for a long moment, heaves a sigh, then launches. "You're all going to Hyperion, a pretty despicable planet known for its unsavory inhabitants. The males will be forced into the arena to fight in pairs—not to the death, mind you. But serious fights that will be wagered on. The captain will take a percentage of the book money, then sell the males to the highest bidder. Then..." he can't maintain eye contact, "then sell the females."

"Sooo, get us impregnated, then separate us from our males and sell us to the highest bidder? Do you agree with this?"

"I've already told you I don't condone any of this. I abhor it. I will go to my grave regretting agreeing to this assignment.

My Lord God, Anteros will never forgive me for this, Anya. This is about the worst thing a Dacian can do, and definitely the worst thing a healer can do." He can't tolerate my angry stare any longer, so he turns to look at the blank wall behind him.

"I would stop it if I could. I am powerless. I'm a healer, not a warrior. Since they brought you females on board, I have barely slept. I've even thought of..."

The pause is so long I wonder if he's hinting he thought of suicide.

"Please." Those deep-set, piercing blue eyes plead with me. "Let me do your exam."

I hop up on the table, totally compliant. This male is in emotional agony. I need say nothing to make him feel worse. He is punishing himself quite competently on his own.

"Shower?" I ask, knowing he won't deny me.

"Absolutely, Miss Anya. Please be brief."

As soon as the lights go out, I attack Zar. There are definite benefits to sharing a tiny bunk with the galaxy's sexiest lion-man. Every time we come together, it gets hotter.

Because the ship took a hit, I assume fixing the overnight lights in the cell block was a low priority. There's one small light at the end of the hall, so it's almost pitch black in our cell. This makes me way more comfortable with what I want to do.

I'm pretty sure Zar can smell my arousal, because I hear him quietly untying his loincloth as I remove my clothes. We're both standing, facing each other near the bed. His hands skim from my waist to the swell of my breasts. He rests their weight in the palms of his hands. I hear his sharp intake of breath. My body is already responding, feeling tight pinpricks of need in the pit of my stomach—and below. Not only does his touch set me on fire, but the sound of his breath hitching, knowing I have this effect on him, escalates my own desires.

He thumbs my nipples, back and forth, slowly. I respond with the softest possible "Mmmm," released from the back of my throat as I tip my head back. When he plucks my nipples, hard, each tug sparks a current of electricity from nipple to clit. My core clenches, already damp in preparation for what's going to come next.

Slipping his hands around my waist, he lifts me as if I weigh nothing. I tighten my legs around his waist. Oh, this is interesting. I feel his soft fur brushing between my legs—what a sensual sensation. My clit rubs against his velvety pelt. I press my breasts against his furred chest and a blast of lust makes my channel clench. The sensation is so erotic, so unique. Like nothing I've ever felt before.

His tail gently encircles my waist as his hard cock bobs between my legs. He's definitely ready for action, but he seems content right now just to kiss me. Long, deep, lingering kisses. His tongue presses between my lips and into my mouth.

It's as if he's charting new territory, getting to know every intimate detail of me—the roof of my mouth, the scrape of my teeth, the texture of my tongue. And then the tip of his tongue spars with the tip of mine. I hadn't realized how many sensitive receptors are on that area, but my nipples tighten even more, and dampness leaks from my core.

He withdraws from my mouth and moves to the curve of my neck, kissing and scraping gently with the points of his sharp canines. "Yeah, that spot," I urge him. He takes direction well because he gives endless attention there. His hot breath mixed with that raspy tongue and those sharp teeth make me impatient.

"Here?" He breathes, then puts his palms on the globes of my ass and presses me against him even harder. My core is spread open against his belly. I'm certain he can feel my wetness through his fur. I writhe on him. Scenting him with my liquid, my passion.

This is the exact moment something unleashes in me. I feel primitive. The soft kisses and caresses that satisfied a moment ago disappear. I'm ramped up, like a feral animal. I bite his neck, where it meets the muscles of his shoulder, scraping the tendons with my teeth.

"Do you smell me, Zar?" I breathe warmly into his ear. "Can you smell how hot you make me? Can you feel just how much I want you? How ready I am?"

"I smell you. I feel your wet heat." His words are whispered, slow, as if he can barely pay attention to anything but his body—and mine.

He shifts me in his arms, moving me further down his body. When he snugs me against him, my clit and dripping slit are now riding his engorged cock. He slides me up and down him.

"Oh my God! Fuck! So good, Zar." My little nub pulses in excitement. Once or twice more of that particular move will make me orgasm right here.

"I'm so open for you, Zar. I want to give you all of me."

My hands are mindlessly roaming from the rock-hard ropey muscles of his shoulders to the indents on the sides of his firm ass. I press him to me even more tightly. The root of his cock bumps my slippery clit. I can hardly bear the desperate desire I'm feeling.

"You're killing me, Zar. I'm so empty. Fill me."

"I'm in charge, Little One. I'm going to kill you slower."

Tipping my head back, I pant in need. I push his head down and lean back, secure in his arms and tail. I want his mouth, those fangs, on my breasts, my nipples. He instantly obliges, dipping his head to focus on a pebbled peak, sucking and scraping with his blunt front teeth. Softly at first, then harder until I lose my mind.

He opens his jaw wide so his fangs are fully exposed. I can feel what he's doing more than see it. His long, sharp canines, two top and two bottom, capture the side of my breast. Not hard. I know with one hundred percent certainty he will not hurt me. The points of his teeth scrape along the tender skin of my breast—like four exquisite pinpricks—then move from the swell of my breast to the tip.

It is the borderline between pleasure and pain. I wonder if he's left a mark. In the darkness, I imagine four thin lines of blood trickling along my pale skin. I have no idea if I'm bleeding, but the idea feels erotic to me. I've been so independent my entire life prior to this. The idea of being marked by him consumes me. He closes his mouth and licks me—four times, slowly—along each of the lines his teeth just scraped.

My core is clenching and quivering. That little moment when you're almost over the precipice into orgasm and every fiber of your being is hurtling toward release.

When he pulls away, I hope we're moving the playing field to the bed. He lays me down, and with feline grace, he practically dives between my legs. I'm so wet and ready. I don't want slow and sweet. I want hard and fast. He licks his finger and slips it between my legs. With his thumb circling my clit, he slides his finger into my wet core. That lovely finger begins a slow rhythm and is soon joined by a second.

My channel quivers, not in orgasm, but arousal. After grabbing his shoulders for leverage, I thrust my hips up to receive more pressure with each powerful drive. His fingers move inside and soon he's rubbing my G-spot in a quick rhythm.

With the force of a hurricane, my orgasm barrels down on me. My fingernails rake his back, breaking skin even through his fur. My inner muscles clamp down in endless waves on his fingers.

He barely gives me time to catch my breath when he thrusts his cock into me—all the way to the hilt in one forceful move. Oh, cock trumps fingers any day! I love the feeling of being stretched, accommodating his girth. He pumps, at first horizontally against me, then adjusting himself until his length and pubic bone hit me just right and I spiral into hyperdrive.

"Oh God," I whisper. "Right there." He needs no instruction. My words are more like high praise. It doesn't take many thrusts before I hurtle over the top again, having another powerful orgasm, my internal muscles vigorously milking his cock. My inner muscles clench and release endlessly. Their rhythm slows, and just when I think the peak is over, he almost imperceptibly changes his angle, increases his pace, and I'm overcome with another wave of delicious spasms.

He must realize I won't be able to physically tolerate another iteration of this because he bends toward me and presses his lips to mine just as he reaches his release. Forcefully thrusting a few more times, he allows a soft grunt to escape his lips, then lies on top of me.

He's careful to keep most of his weight on knees and forearms—just enough for me to feel covered and safe. He snuggles his face against my neck, and my attention moves from the delicious aftershocks of my inner walls still clenching to the fact that his whiskers tickle.

I giggle and move to scoot out from under him. When he realizes what's going on, he puts more weight on me and deliberately scruffs my neck with them. I giggle some more.

We play this silly game for a moment more, until he slides his back to the wall and pulls me close. I only have a moment to reflect on the amazing, life-changing sex we just exchanged in this little cell, then fall asleep.

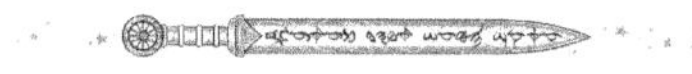

ANYA!

It's Tyree. I don't know how long she's been calling me. I blush, wondering how much of our lovemaking she's been aware of.

Yes, I'm awake.

Good news! She sounds over-the-top excited.

What?

I'm right outside your cell. It's probably time you introduce me to Zar.

I peek through the bars and see her tiny form in the shadows. I put my finger over Zar's lips so he doesn't make any noise when I awaken him. "Zar," I whisper, "Tyree is here."

His muscles instantly tighten, going into emergency mode until his brain comprehends my words, then he follows my gaze and nods.

"Can you hear her talking to you in your head?"

He stills, head cocked slightly as he listens intently, then shakes his head. "I hear nothing."

What's the news, Tyree? I ask.

I got the captain to eat Sillerian worms.

I have no response to this.

You have no idea how big this is, Anya. The captain hates Sillerian worms. He will rant about how awful they are and how he can't understand why they're such a popular delicacy across the galaxy. I not only had him eat the worms, I had him ask for seconds. He's in his bed right now moaning in agony. Those worms don't agree with him. Tyree sounds triumphant.

This is huge! I agree. *If you got him to do that, do you think you can force him to turn our collars off?*

Yes! Yes, I do. She gloats, then her tone changes. *I don't know how long I can sustain it. But I can do it.*

That's the best news I've had all day. I pause to fill Zar in on the conversation.

First Axxios and now this, we've overcome our two biggest problems. I'm more confident than ever.

Tyree steps out of the shadows, and I look at her for the first time since we met the night of my arrival.

"Tyree, are you sick?" I whisper.

Why do you ask? She inquires in my head.

It's hard to see in the dim light, but your features seem... different. You seem different. I can't put my finger on it. *Maybe it's just the shadows,* I hedge.

I've been feeling... odd. My psychic powers have grown by leaps and bounds recently. Other things have felt weird, too. I've been achy. I have no idea what's going on.

Have you talked to Dr. Drayke about it?

No. Maybe I should.

I fill Zar in on the rest of our conversation after Tyree leaves. He seems concerned about her, worried her health might affect the rebellion. My brows knit in anxiety as I brood about it. Not only do I care about her, but without her, there can be no revolution.

Chapter Eleven

Tyree

I take seldom-used back hallways on my way to the captain's room. I know every hidey-hole and storage area I can dodge into in case someone sees me. There is no room or bunk for me on this ship. I'm just a pet who lives in the captain's room, a thing to be tolerated. On the other hand, my non-status gives me a lot of freedom of movement and almost no expectations from the crew. Gods forbid, though, if I'm not available for the captain when he has use of me.

I jump to place my palm on the touchscreen lock to get into "my" quarters. I scramble into the bathroom and climb up to sit on the counter, my knees straddling the sink to look into the mirror above it.

The sheer panic in Anya's voice forced me to quit ignoring my inner warnings and take a good look at myself. And oh my, she was right. Something is off, way off. I balance on my knees, one on each of the narrow edges of the sink. Kneeling, I lean closer to the mirror and inspect my face.

The normally rounded, almost childlike look of my cheeks is somehow more angular. My chin is slightly more pro-nounced. My jade green eyes look dull and have almost lost their glow from within. This confirms my recent feeling that I've developed a low-grade fever.

I jump down from the sink and quickly shuck my leggings. Holy *drack*, my usually childlike thighs and calves are taking on muscular definition. My hands look... bigger.

Completely distracted, functioning on impulse, I drag my clothes back on my body, almost pulling my pants on backward. It can't be happening. It just can't. My stomach clenches and seems to sink.

It's funny how a person can think they are sane and calm and reasonable and believe it all their life until faced with a reality they don't want to accept. I've been acting like a delusional schoolgirl these past few days as I avoid the obvious.

The Transformation.

There, I said it. The Transformation, I say it again inside my head and then, "The Transformation," I speak it out loud just to bludgeon my brain into believing it.

I was born on planet Larian many *annums* ago, to a family of moderate means. We lived simply on a modest farm outside of a small town. My race hadn't developed anything near computers or the ability to travel in space. We used a wheeled cart drawn by muscular, four-legged *ortoni* to travel for supplies. It was on one of these trips that I learned about the Transformation.

I had a friend, Morley, a youngling who didn't look any older than me, who was the child of the general store's owners. I loved going into town, not just because the store owners always gave me a stick of delicious *manu* candy, but because I enjoyed playing with Morley.

I was young enough I had never really asked questions about males and females. I knew that parents were men and women, and I just assumed that kids were kids. The idea of gender never really interested me.

One day we arrived in town for provisions, and I didn't see Morley. When I asked Morley's father where she was, he looked surprised and immediately glanced at my parents as if to ask for their guidance.

It was then that I saw a tall, muscular adult male brooding quietly at the table in the corner where the townspeople sometimes came to play cards on wintry days. He was staring intently at me.

My parents looked shocked, maybe even a bit fearful, and ordered me to wait in the wagon outside. My folks were kind and loving and seldom raised their voices to me. I was shy and compliant, well I guess I still am, and ran to wait in the back of the wagon.

I'd never seen our order filled or our wagon loaded so quickly. The ride back to our farm was swift and silent.

That night at dinner, my parents explained the Transformation. Frankly, it made my head spin. They explained how Larians were born with no gender and could stay that way their whole lives. They remained genderless until they found their truemate. At that time, one member of the couple became female and the other became male. The individuals could be any age, from twenty to sixty—childbearing *annums*.

My parents explained it was a mystery how the body changed, going in a matter of <u>days</u> from a tiny, childlike being to towering muscular males who were over six *fiertos* tall, or statuesque females with curves and breasts. They didn't understand how the vents used for excreting became external for males or internal for females, or how men then produced sperm and females produced eggs. It was simply inscrutable.

I pressed them with questions about how I would know when I met my truemate, how it was decided. The whole sex and genitals part was simply too gross and unbelievable, so my young mind latched onto the personal connection. How would I meet this person? How would I know? How was it decided which of the pair became male and which became female?

To my parents' credit, they gave me no meaningful answers because they had no answers to give. They simply had no way of knowing. Our science was crude. There were no facts in any book to explain things. I've snuck onto the captain's computer many times, searching for information, but there are no other species in the known universe that reproduce like this, so there's no research on it.

I only saw Morley once more after his Transformation. We went into town for his Joining Ceremony. I had met his mate once at the shoemaker's shop. Now she looked tall and regal and very grown up.

I sought Morley out, but he wasn't particularly interested in me. He had a mate and was now interested in far more adult things than an old playmate. He had seemed so distracted that later, on the ride home, I asked my parents about it. Now, as they explained everything they could, they alluded to his growing paranormal powers.

They said not all Larians grew special powers when their body transitioned, but some did. Some could hear others' thoughts, some could move items with just a desire, some could feel others' emotions. They denied that either of them had acquired any additional powers upon their Transformations, then laughed and said maybe it had "skipped a generation" and I would develop lots of powers just like grandfather Crantu. I never got much of an answer from them about what those capabilities might be.

I was kidnapped from my planet not too long after that. So, my trove of knowledge is pitifully small. By my reckoning, I'm thirty-five *annums* of age. I never figured I would hit my Transformation because I never thought I'd see another Larian. I had taken it as fact that my Transformation could be triggered only by another of my kind.

But, as I look down and see muscular legs where before there had been childlike, undefined meat on bone, I can't deny my Transformation has been triggered. And it must have been triggered by someone on board.

All the gladiators and females seem to be paired up. I can't imagine who it could be. It can't be the captain, the doctor, or the other members of the crew, or I would have changed long before now. I'm excited and terrified and totally baffled.

Anya

The next morning, along with the command to complete the act, we are cheerfully informed the captain has declared today a "holiday" to celebrate our defeat of the Marauders. We women are invited to watch the males in gladiatorial competition. Oh, happy day.

What makes him believe the males want to compete, especially in front of us? And I doubt any of us women want to watch. From what I'd observed the day the Marauders attacked, none of the women would want to watch their males get hurt.

When I glance at Zar, however, I realize I got at least half of the equation wrong. He looks thrilled! Totally pumped.

"You'll watch me fight today, Anya? You'll see me fight. You'll see me win!"

When did he become a monosyllabic caveman, I wonder. Then I remember he's a gladiator. He's done this his whole life. It's the one thing he thinks he's good at. Of course he wants to show off for his female.

Prizefighting on TV is something I've never enjoyed. I couldn't bear to even glance at World Wide Wrestling when scrolling through the channels, even though it was obviously fake as hell. I definitely know I don't want to see my guy getting hit and possibly bloodied in a show for my entertainment.

Then I glance at his expectant face. He's like a five-year-old who just picked the neighbor's flowers and presents them excitedly to his Mom expecting enthusiasm and praise.

"Can't wait," I say, faking sincerity.

We do our business quickly with mutual pleasure, and I'm escorted to medbay. Dr. Drayke seems enthused about the upcoming exhibition.

"Really?" I ask. "You didn't seem the type."

"These men train for this all day every day. To be able to have an audience, without the fear of..." He interrupts his train of thought, not wanting to mention that usually these events don't allow the males the luxury of knowing they'll emerge in one piece. "Well, at any rate, this should be a safe way for them to swagger in front of their females."

"Hmmm... I'm curious, doc, you talk to every woman every day. How many of these women have... paired up with their males?"

"Paired up?" He looks confused.

"How many of my fellow ladies are kind of happy with their cellmates?"

"Anya, I don't have long conversations with the other fe-males. I have no idea what goes on in their heads. I can tell you, though, most of them don't look nearly as unhappy now as they did on their first day. None seem to have what might be called 'failure to thrive.' A few have begun to ask if they could already be pregnant."

Wham! It suddenly hits me that I've been so preoccupied with the insurrection I've completely pushed the question of a possible pregnancy to the back of my mind like a child pushes their dreaded peas to the back of their plate.

"You could tell already?"

"Of course."

I guess I should have known this. "Test me!" It's an order.

"I do test you, Miss Anya. I test each of you every day."

"And?"

"I haven't examined you yet today, but no, you weren't as of yesterday."

My mind completely shuts down. I have no idea whether I'm happy or sad about this news. At this moment, I can't even connect with my emotions.

"Is that good news or bad?" he asks.

"I don't know," I mumble, my lips numb.

Chapter Twelve

Zar

We're given our sparring assignments and I nod formally to Dax, who I'm paired with. Since I fight as a murmillo, it is fitting that I fight a retiarius Gladiator. We are commonly matched in combat.

We all get to work, lifting weights, running a bit, warming up before the females enter. I notice a few of the males begin to preen. Following their gaze to what has been set aside as the viewing area, I see the women taking seats on mats on the floor.

I catch Anya's eye. She's biting her lower lip, her brows knit together in worry. I realize she must be anxious about me. Did she not believe me when I told her I'm the best gladiator in the *ludus?* This is just an exhibition. I give her a thumbs-up sign and an open smile showing my fangs. I hope she understands it means don't worry about me, this will be fun.

"I am Doctoré, the head of this *ludus*, or gladiator school," Doctoré's sonorous voice commands attention from all. I respect him completely. He is tall and thin, his skin a dark burnished ebony. His face, though humanoid, is thin and elongated. The skin on his shoulder and pectoral are pebbled.

He is strong, sage, and completely fair. Looking at his proud bearing, if you didn't know he was a slave, you'd think he was a ruler from a distant planet. He's taught me a lot, even though I've known him for such a short time and I've trained under many other teachers. The difference? Doctoré actually cares about us.

"Our revered captain has granted you the honor of watching several sparring matches in this exhibition. These males are well trained and excited to perform for you. Do not fret, other than a few nicks and scrapes, this display of strength and prowess is designed for entertainment only and none of these fine males will be harmed in the proceedings."

Anya's shoulders relax a tiny bit. She still looks worried, her bottom lip captured in her top teeth. This gives me a warm feeling inside. She's the first person since Pallatin to genuinely care whether I live or die.

The nine other females are sitting on the floor of the *ludus*. The blue doctor, the Urluts, and the first mate are all here. The captain and little Tyree must be watching through holo-vid on the bridge. It makes sense. Someone needs to be at the helm.

Shadow edges over to me and whispers, "We should attack now."

Had we known this was going to happen, this might very well have been a good time to attack. We have our weapons and some crude shields. The Urluts will certainly be distracted by the fight. They love to gamble and will be more focused on betting than on guarding any of us.

"We're not prepared. We don't know if Tyree is watching and can deactivate the collars. We haven't organized our plan of attack, and most importantly, the females are easy targets and would certainly be attacked by the cowardly guards."

"As I said before," Shadow says contemptuously, "your feelings about that female have made you soft."

"It may well be, Shadow, but none of the other males will be willing to risk their females' lives. Did you see how possessive they were when we cleaned up after the Marauder attack? You might be running forward with your sword drawn, but none of us will be behind you. No one will have your back." I wait, hoping my words sink in. "The right time is coming, Shadow, and it will be soon. But not today."

Shadow grunts in response, obviously not happy, but seeing my logic.

Doctoré continues, "The first match will be between Steele and Axxios. Our way of fighting these matches goes back millennia. We have specific categories of ceremonial fighters, each with its own history, its own weapons, each with its own shields. Steele and Axxios will both be fighting as cestus gladiators. It is tradition that cestus gladiators wear no clothing."

A small titter erupts from the women. I noticed shortly after we met that little Anya seemed embarrassed to show her body. It seems these humans all have prohibitions against nudity. They'll be in for a show during this match.

Steele steps forward and unceremoniously removes his loincloth. His silver body is already covered in a sheen of sweat from his warm-up. Axxios, our golden gladiator pilot, removes his loincloth, managing to look for all the galaxy as if he is taking off the finest overcoat at a fancy ball.

They square off in the designated area.

"Cestus gladiators are not allowed weapons or shields of any kind. These matches are usually a warm-up before the bigger contests that are to come," Doctoré explains.

I've watched these two spar since we've been on this ship together. I know they are evenly matched. First impressions might make a novice believe Axxios will be the certain winner. His body is so much thicker, so much more heavily muscled, that I imagine if the females were gamblers, they would bet on him to win.

My eyes travel to Zoey, Steele's tiny mate. I noticed the other day she is extremely fearful and shy. She never worked up the nerve to even look at me, much less give me eye contact. Now she appears practically paralyzed with dread. She must have jumped to the conclusion her cellmate will be beaten badly.

Axxios's female, Brianna, I think her name is, looks confident. I think she's trying to act as if she's uninterested and completely above this whole affair, but I can see that isn't true. Her gaze is glued on Axxios.

"Begin," Doctoré calls.

The men thump their fists lightly on their chests and nod to their opponent as is custom. After approaching each other warily, Axxios rushes Steele. They grapple each other, necks straining, muscles bulging. They are grunting, shoving, struggling, trying to push each other onto the ground.

As I thought, Axxios is not the easy victor. Steele, although he doesn't have Axxios's obvious bulk, is lithe, strong, and quicker on his feet. It's an excellent match of talents.

I'm surprised when I steal a glance at the females. They don't appear to be appreciating this contest. Most are watching in horror, if at all. Zoey looks as if she's about to faint—her eyes look huge in her pale face. I hope neither male in the ring glances over at their females. They would peek over to catch the appreciation in their females' eyes and be distracted when they see the women are repulsed by the display.

Finally, Axxios wrestles Steele to the floor. Both their bodies hit the mat with such force the loud noise gathers everyone's attention. It looks as if Axxios is winning when he begins to press Steele's silver shoulders to the mat.

Before Doctoré can call the match, Steele flips himself off the mat and almost sits on Axxios's shoulders, the bigger man still down on all fours. Steele brilliantly levers his body weight to push Axxios forward and down, using all his might to press Axxios's shoulders to the mat. Doctoré hollers, "Ho! Match to Steele."

The gladiators all stomp their left feet on the floor, a show of appreciation to both men, especially to Steele for a match well fought. Axxios claps Steele on the upper arm, the etiquette of the ring to admit defeat.

The women, at first speechless, clap politely, obviously more dismayed than impressed. I silently caution myself not to look over at Anya during my match. Obviously, on her planet there is no appreciation for this type of combat. I can't blame her. From everything she's told me she came from a backwater planet that didn't even have fully functional space travel, how could they be expected to enjoy a spectacle this advanced?

"Zar and Dax," Doctoré announces.

I take a moment to glance over at Anya and she looks stricken. She referred to Dax as, what was it, a Neanderthal? I don't know what that means, but she didn't seem to want to get to know the male. He's nice enough. He has also been a slave most of his life. He's lived and trained in rougher places than I. I learned a few manners about eating and hygiene over the *annums* that I don't think he was privileged to receive. He is a man of few words, but I've never known him to be anything but kind.

When Dax and I square off, I realize what might have upset Anya. Dax is big. Really big. He is taller than me by a head and definitely outweighs me. His muscles seem more pronounced, but probably because he has skin like my Anya, and I have fur. My fur might hide some of my muscles.

Dax is a retiarius, which means he fights with a long spear with a trident point—three blades at the end. Of course, we are only fighting with wooden replicas. He's also equipped with a net, big enough to cast at me. It's designed to disable me or trip me up.

As a murmillo gladiator, I have a three-*fierto* blade, also wooden, and a large rectangular shield. Through the ages, these two types of gladiators were supposed to be well matched. There are advantages to each. Dax's weapons are built for longer reach. His trident is almost three times longer than my sword. His net can be used in many cunning methods, and his gear weighs much less than mine, which gives him speed and agility.

My sword, however, is designed to disable my opponent much more effectively than his spear. Once I get close enough to my opponent, his trident becomes ineffective, while my sword becomes deadly. Besides, I've sparred with Dax for weeks. He's not as swift or nimble as I am.

I know who will be the inevitable winner of this match, but Anya doesn't. I glance over at her and see her jaw is clenched, her brow knitted—her fear is palpable. I give her a smile and the thumbs-up sign again. She takes a deep breath, but I don't think I've reassured her.

Anya

Holy shit. I am completely beside myself with worry. I can hardly comprehend what is going on in the ring, and I have absolutely no time or energy to process the fact that this confirms the whole *Chariots of the Gods* idea. Most experts considered the book a conspiracy theory. The author said aliens visited Earth millennia ago and possibly seeded the planet with offshoots of their race. Some related theories said other aliens visited and provided some of their culture as well as their DNA.

What else would explain the fact that the ancient Romans had the exact same fighters and combat styles as what I'm watching two thousand years later and a trillion miles away?

I have no time to ponder this. Back to the business at hand, which is that my lion guy is going to be caught in a net by an enormous caveman and poked into submission by a seven-foot spear.

My heart is thumping so hard I can barely hear the Urluts' raucous cheers. Dax throws his net, trying to trip Zar. He patiently pulls it back and casts it again and again, effectively keeping Zar away from him. Zar's weapon isn't long enough to do any damage at all. He's too far away to strike his opponent, and with no sharp edge on his wooden sword, he can't cut the net.

Dax seems to have finally tired Zar out. Zar looks winded, and his movements seem slower. The bigger male is about to throw the spear, which looks dangerous even though it's wooden, when Zar moves swift and sure. He approaches his opponent and slams the side of the sword with tremendous force against Dax's midsection. It hits him with such violence that the big guy expels his breath in a huff. It knocked the air out of him, because for a brief moment he almost doubles over. Then he stands tall again, but I can tell he's gasping to draw breath.

Zar sees his opening and steps forward again, battering Dax in the same spot again. Dax wobbles. You can see a slashing red welt forming on his skin. Dax is still not recovered when Zar smashes him yet again with the blunt side of the sword. This time, Dax loses his breath and hits the mat with his knees—hard.

With Zar in close next to Dax, the caveman is at a severe disadvantage. He can't throw his net, and the long spear is useless at such close range. Dax makes a valiant effort to choke up on the spear to get his grip closer to the pointed end so he can thrust with it, but he's no match for Zar's swift, catlike grace.

Zar moves behind the big man, puts what would be the cutting edge of the sword against Dax's throat, and looks toward Doctoré to see if the match is over. Doctoré nods and announces, "Ho! Match to Zar."

I hadn't realized, but somewhere during that fight I rose to my feet, one hand over my mouth to keep from crying out. Now that Zar is safe, I realize how consumed I'd been. I gasp in a gulp of air, wondering how long I'd been holding my breath.

My knees feel weak now that the match is over. What if that fight had been for real? Zar could have been killed. Dax could have been killed. I look down and see that I bit my knuckle until it bled while I was watching the match.

It suddenly strikes me, more clearly than I'd have believed possible, that this has been Zar's world his whole life. This is Zar's "normal." It's as natural as breathing for him to train, to fight, and to kill.

I can't help but think of him in a new light. At first, my mind flies into worry mode. How can I have feelings for this man—a stone-cold killer? Then I calm a bit and realize this is who he's been groomed to be. This is who he's been forced to be. His whole world has been kill or be killed, and he was smart and athletic enough to be on the winning, living, breathing end of that equation.

But the male I share a cell with, that's the real Zar. When no one is threatening his life, when it's just two people alone in a room, that's the male he wants to be, the one who lives in his heart. The authentic person who inhabits that gorgeous, muscular body is the person who apologized for what he was forced to do to me in bed. It's that person who doesn't want to eat half of my rations. It is that person who is willing to risk his life to lead this rebellion—not so much because he wants it, but because it's what I want.

I know Zar's heart, and it is good. I love this man. I had toyed with the idea for the last few days. I kept telling myself it was the whole falling-in-love-because-there's-danger thing. But at this very moment, I realize not only do I love Zar. I love him for all the right reasons.

I can tell Zar's eyes are on me throughout the next few matches. He looks quizzical, then his brows slash in worry. I assume he's trying to read my mind. I wonder if he thinks I'm sickened by the barbarous behavior I just witnessed.

I'm staring at him not because I'm repelled, but because I'm so compellingly attracted to him. I can't look him in the eyes right now. I just can't.

Zar

Something's going on with Anya and it's not good. She won't even look at me. I must disgust her. Seeing the real me, the me who is trained to fight and win and kill, has repulsed her. Why wouldn't it? She grew up on a peaceful planet with parents who loved her and safeguarded her and gave her a room to sleep in with a door that locked for her protection.

She's never had to fight for scraps to eat. She's never had to plot and make alliances and take advantage of others' weaknesses. She has never, until a few short days ago, worried that her life might end at any moment. Or had to kill someone she loved. How could she look at me as anything other than an absolute barbarian?

Right now I should be watching the bouts. In a few short days, we're going to land on Hyperion and I'll be matched against one of these males in a fight with real weapons, possibly to the death. Even though I've sparred with these gladiators many times, I should be evaluating their strengths and weaknesses. I should be looking for vulnerabilities to exploit in the future when my life may depend on it.

But I can't pay attention to anything other than Anya's beautiful face. I've never seen her other than close up in the cell. Now I can watch her from a distance. She's even lovelier with this span between us. I don't know if I ever noticed her heart-shaped face, the delicate way her eyebrows frame her eyes, or that her neck is as graceful as a dancer's.

My heart hitches in my chest. I can't lose her. I can't lose this female. We can't land on Hyperion. We'll have to make a stand here on this ship. We have to finalize our plans on how to overthrow this vessel, and we must act soon.

Anya

The females are taken back to the cell block first, leaving the males in the *ludus*. I sneak one last look at Zar before they make us leave the makeshift arena. Good Lord, he is so amazingly handsome. He's the perfect merger of man and cat. The ideal combination of hard muscle and soft fur. The splendid union of lithe movement and prodigious strength.

All I can think about is jumping his bones. He is so sexy. His fighting and winning today, rather than scaring me or turning me off, has poured gasoline on my already flaming libido. How am I ever going to wait until lights out?

"Holy shit," Maddie, Stryker's cellmate, exclaims on the way back to our cells. "Is it just me, or was that whole exhibition Hot. As. Hell?" She mock fans herself with her hand.

Every single woman in line laughs, nodding—even Zoey, Steele's timid cellmate.

"Okay," Savannah laughs, "so it's not just me? Good to know."

"There's something to be said for sheer, raw, male power," Callista agrees.

"No talking!" the Urlut shouts as he brandishes his baton.

Silence.

Zar

I'm not sure what to expect when I duck into the cell a short time later. I surely didn't foresee her big smile, or her coming to greet me as soon as the Urluts leave the cell block. She presses her hands to my cheeks and strokes my mane and then pulls back to look me up and down. She circles me slowly and deliberately, as she seems to be reassuring herself that I'm in one piece.

"You fought like a lion today." Then she laughs. When I lift my eyebrow in question, she explains, "On my world, there are animals that look a lot like you. They're called lions."

When I give a skeptical glance, she quickly amends, "They're apex predators in their hunting grounds. They're powerful, beautiful creatures."

I have no idea how to respond to this. Yesterday I looked like some pet in her world. Today I'm like a killing machine?

She draws my attention from these thoughts when she puts her hands on the back of my neck and pulls my lips to hers. Her kisses aren't tentative or sweet or innocent as they've often been before. They are insistent and impatient. Her tongue invades my mouth, her body presses to mine like a second coat of fur. As her luscious breasts press into my midriff, she straddles one of my legs and presses her core against my thigh. I've never seen her this forceful or demanding.

She's riding my thigh, making soft moaning noises in the back of her throat. It doesn't take me long to catch up to the intensity of her desire. I'm instantly hard and ready to take her. She certainly doesn't seem to want or need foreplay.

When she forcefully whispers, "Fuck me, Zar," it dispels any hesitance I may have had.

"The lights," I point out, my voice thick with passion.

"I don't give a fuck about the lights. I don't care who hears. I don't care if there are cameras. I want you. Now."

She's already climbed up on me, her legs wrapped around my waist, her upper arms around my shoulders and her hands sifting through the mane on the back of my head. I hold her hips, my tail encircling her waist.

Her tongue almost savagely explores the cavern of my mouth. I turn us both around and press her back into the far corner of the cell. If the Urluts are watching, all they'll see are my rear and haunches. They won't see my Anya.

I pull my cock out of my loincloth, not even trying to untie the *dracking* thing. While I'm doing that, she drops her feet to the floor, drags her bottoms down, and wiggles them off. Placing her hands on my shoulders, she pulls herself back up and locks her ankles behind my back.

Her level of passion is igniting mine, and I can't get into position fast enough. My cock finds her wet center, needing no help from either of our hands. She's dripping wet and practically writhing on the head of my dick. I pierce into her channel as I groan, seating myself in one exquisite thrust.

Before I can even initiate a rhythm, she begins to move. Her hands are on my shoulders, and she uses her upper body strength to ride me. I take a moment to look at her lovely face. She is so passionate, so intent on the powerful feelings coursing through her. Her head is pressed against the wall as she positions her pelvis next to mine to get the best angle and pressure. I could watch her like this for *hoaras*, but this isn't going to take *hoaras*. She's already close.

She changes her angle almost imperceptibly and I realize this ratchets her passion up a notch. She's moaning louder, pressing harder, breathing faster. I match her rhythm exactly, and her excitement increases to a level I didn't know was possible. I lean down and nip her in the crook between her neck and shoulder and that catapults her over the edge. Her inner walls grip my cock, hard and pulsing, which leads to a cataclysmic orgasm of my own.

Anya

Oh my God. Where did this Anya come from? Holy shit, I've never been here before. I've been horny, yeah, that's nothing new. But attacking someone? Demanding like that? Not caring if the Urluts were watching and jacking off to what we were doing? No, this is a new part of me I've never met before.

My back is still pressed against the hard rear wall of the cell. I'm still impaled on Zar's fabulous cock (which, by the way, is still prodigiously huge and hard). I know at some point I should probably have a long, serious talk with myself and figure out what is going on with my psyche. Perhaps if I was still on Earth, I'd schedule an appointment with a therapist and figure out what things in my childhood contributed to me being vulnerable to this intense attraction to lion-man.

But I'll ponder that later, because, hey, I'd hate to waste this moment, still connected to such a *hot*, handsome, sexy lion-man. I nip him in the harbor where neck meets shoulder, right where he so passionately nipped me. My hips ride him, more slowly this time. If anything, this is more sensual, more passionate than what we experienced a moment ago.

This time, he takes control. He leans down to scrape my already overly sensitive nipples with his blunt front teeth. When he stands back up to his considerable full height, and my nipples press against his suede-like fur, it's one of the most erotic sensations I've ever experienced. I don't know whether to focus on breasts or pussy. At this point, I am incapable of multitasking. I have to choose.

Okay, I choose pussy. Pussy and clit. This ride is delicious as he is not only hitting all the right spots with all the right pressure and all the right friction and just the right movement, but he's found a magic spot *inside* me that almost instantly pushes me over the top. My orgasm triggers his own. He tries to be quiet, but he lets out an appreciative feline hiss.

His essence bathes my inner walls, a testament to his power, his virility. A frisson of fear spikes through me when I realize sperm can make babies, but I can't worry about that right now. I'm in Zar's powerful arms as he nuzzles my cheek.

"Anya." Using his burred tongue, he laps the corner of my mouth with affection. "Mine," he growls.

I'm incapable of thought or movement for a few moments. My inner walls are still quivering with aftershocks. If we were in a bed in a locked room, I'd be ready for round three in about a minute. But the reality that the Urluts probably *are* jacking off to our video feed finally penetrates my foggy brain.

Zar senses the change in me and, still managing to cover my nudity, he leans to retrieve my bottoms. After helping me step into them, he maneuvers himself back into his loincloth. We walk the few steps to the bed and settle in under the blanket. He pets my hair, his eyes never leaving mine.

We both give a startled laugh when we hear the undeniable sound of a male orgasm grunting from down the hall. We're still enjoying the unspoken joke when we hear a female trying to stifle a scream of passion.

"Do you think the Urluts gave us an aphrodisiac?" he asks seriously, cocking his head.

How do I explain that the primitive gladiatorial exhibition, which one week ago would have repulsed me, was a bigger turn-on than a room full of Chippendale dancers? Thunder from Down Under can't compete with seeing all that muscular man-flesh sparring in the arena. Who knew?

"I think seeing our men fighting was exciting... I know it was for me," I say shyly. Why I'm shy now, I have no idea. I certainly wasn't shy a few minutes ago when I practically jumped my cellmate.

"Perhaps I will never understand human females."

"Maybe that's a good thing, babe."

Chapter Thirteen

ANYA

It's after lights out and I still hear sounds of sex echoing up and down the hallway. Zar and I have a lot of organizing to do. I call Tyree through our telepathic connection—it's faster than email!

She makes her way quickly to the cell block and soon we're communicating in person, though still through our telepathic link.

How are you feeling? I ask. I've been pretty worried about her. She looked like shit when I last saw her.

I think I'm coming down with something.

Is she hedging, I wonder?

Should you see Dr. Drayke?

It will pass. I'm just under the weather.

I peer into the darkness, trying to get a better look at her.

Tyree, if anything I think you look worse. Will you promise to talk to Dr. Drayke?

Long pause. I have enough of a psychic connection to get a clear impression she's withholding something from me.

Anya, I don't think he can help me. I promise I'll talk to him if I need help.

It's like she pulls an iron shutter down, immediately severing the connection between us. She's never done that before. I believe her powers *are* growing by leaps and bounds. This has to be good news for our rebellion.

Okay, I'm just worried about you. I can feel her open the line of communication again.

I promise I'm fine and this will not interfere with our plans. We land on Hyperion in a few days. When are we going to try this overthrow? I think the timing will be important.

Yes, I agree, I nod, not sure if she can even see me. *The males will be in the ludus. They can't start the attack until the collars are disabled, but how will they know you've accomplished that?*

I've been pondering that myself. I have to develop a connection with one of the males. A good enough link that I can reach them from my spot on the bridge all the way to the ludus *on a lower level of the ship.*

Who?

No idea, she answers forlornly, lips pressed tight.

Why don't you go up and down the hall and see if any of them can hear you? Then I listen intently, trying to notice if any of the other couples are still engaged in lustful activities. That would be awkward!

I think all is clear, she answers my unspoken question. *I'll try it right now.*

Tyree

I try again to establish a connection with Zar. I know him, feel somewhat comfortable with him, and he doesn't scare me as much as the others. But he doesn't even stir.

Then I begin down the line of cells toward the far end of the hallway. I try at each cell, but no luck.

I make my way back down the hallway toward the exit. When I pass Anya's cell again, she asks, *So? Anything encouraging?*

I shake my head, then move toward the last two cells on my way out. I pause in front of Grace and Shadow's cell. Shadow, frankly, scares the *drack* out of me. He's one of the hardest, most brutal, and callous males I have ever met.

I don't allow my thoughts to connect with the Urluts, they are simply too brutish for me to tolerate even the smallest psychic interaction. So, other than the Urluts, Shadow is the harshest male I've ever encountered. Worse even than the captain.

I tamp down my fear, knowing I have to try every possible avenue, which means attempting to connect with him. First, though, I watch him and Grace from the dim light of my hiding place.

Dr. Drayke found Grace some clothes shortly after her arrival. It was one of his own blue jumpsuits. The legs and arms were way too long, so they're rolled up at the ankles and wrists. The rest of the suit is still huge on her. Her form looks like a blue blob. But at least she has a modicum of dignity and isn't running around almost nude.

I mostly avoid this cell like the Zonarian plague because of Shadow's cruel energy, so today I pay attention to Grace almost for the first time. She's really pretty. She's not tiny like me, but she's the smallest of the Earth females.

She seems so unhappy! I certainly understand why. I wouldn't be able to tolerate living in that tiny cell with Shadow.

I begin telepathically calling Shadow's name, softly at first, then louder. I quickly know he's getting my signal. At first, he sits up in his bunk. Then he looks around, confused. Then he stands, comes to the front bars of the cell, and peers directly at me even though I thought I was hidden in the darkness.

"What's going on?" he questions angrily.

I'm Tyree. I'm talking to you in your mind. Can you hear me? It's a ridiculous question, I realize immediately.

"Yes, I can hear you!" He's talking pretty loud. Is he not afraid of the guards?

Talk back to me in your head, I practically order him. The last thing either of us needs is to be discovered plotting together.

Who are you to order me around? He demands, but at least his lips aren't moving and he's not verbalizing his bossy commands out loud.

As I said, I have no idea where I got the nerve, but I'm trying to get the upper hand with this hostile barbarian. *I'm Tyree. I'm the one who's going to get the collars disabled.*

And? He challenges arrogantly.

And, I answer back haughtily, *I need one of you gladiators to hear my thoughts so you'll know when the collars are disabled and you can start fighting.*

This seems to put him in his place. I can feel him back off from his aggressive stance and cooperate with me.

So, it's obvious you can receive my thoughts. Obvious, too, that you can send, I say, more than ready to terminate the conversation.

His belligerent energy is soul-sucking. *I'll try to connect with you in half an* hoara *from the bridge. Let me know if you receive my thoughts. Tomorrow I'll connect with you in the* ludus. *If that works, we'll be much closer to taking over the ship.*

Fine, is all he says dismissively, then stalks back to his bunk.

I take a glance at Grace, who can't hear either of us, but is aware something is going on. I spare a quick moment to pity her. She's the only female on the cell block who hasn't made some peace with her situation. Her misery is palpable. I send her calming and healing energy, not knowing if she has the capacity to receive it. But her body jolts as if something got through to her. I see her shoulders relax in the dim light. Perhaps I gave her some comfort.

Anya

Tyree doubled back to give me the good news that Shadow is our new go-between. Neither of us speaks the obvious, which is that although he is the best qualified psychically, he is the worst qualified temperamentally. Oh well, we'll take what we can get.

Zar receives this news with excitement. "Anya, all the big problems are out of the way." He's practically crowing with satisfaction. "We just have to hammer out the details and we'll be ready."

We put our heads together as we kneel on the floor in front of the bed. Although his mouth is inches from my ear, I can barely hear him, because he's whispering so quietly. We trace our fingers on the thin surface of the blanket, drawing hallways and schematics with nothing more than fingertips and imagination.

Luckily, the males are well acquainted with the layout of the ship since they were shown the way to the bridge during the Marauder attack.

Over and over again we ask each other questions. With each "what if," we struggle for an answer or a logical workaround. Each time we review, we get down to smaller and smaller details.

Who should receive the first weapon? Zar has fangs and claws, Shadow has prosthetics that are stronger than flesh, Axxios and Dax are gargantuan and innately strong. Steele, Zar points out to me, has almost as few natural protections as humans. He would be a force to be reckoned with if he had a laser.

Who should run point as they proceed from the *ludus* to the bridge? We arrange a clear hierarchy for that. When should the women be included? Never—we both agree. We will be safest in our little cell block. We'll have to trust the males. This wasn't an easy decision to come to. Trust is not my strong point.

Then we get down to the nitty-gritty of "the list" as I've been calling it in my mind. Talk about playing God. We are writing a list of who shall live and who shall die. How very Old Testament of us.

It doesn't turn out to be as difficult as it sounds. We come up with plan A and plan B. Plan A is to try to kill no one but the Urluts. The other people need to be subdued and put in the same cells we're currently confined to while we figure out what to do with them. Plan B, though, is that if challenged, keeping the gladiators alive and safe is priority number one. If one of our enemies does not stand down, they will have to be... terminated.

I'm not super happy about this, but it's logical and they haven't exactly treated us like BFFs.

Then we get to the little issue of Dr. Drayke sun Omrun. At first, Zar advocates for his death. Upon discussion, however, I discover he mostly wants Dr. Drayke dead because he's been intimately acquainted with my lady parts.

I remind him the doc has been helpful and basically kind. He tried to make the invasive exams as painless and quick as possible. He feels remorse, and since it looks like we're going to be on this ship for a while, it would be nice to have a real doctor in medbay. Ultimately, Zar grudgingly agrees to let the poor guy live.

Zar and I briefly discuss the elephant in the room, which is what we are going to do after the revolution. If we lose, there is no problem—we'll all be dead or sold into slavery and will have absolutely no decisions to make. If we win, well, that's the big question.

We'll have ten gladiators, ten Earth women, and a few stragglers from the original crew. That's over twenty mouths to feed. We have no idea how to find the money to pay for fuel or food. We'll be homeless, with no welcoming planet to go to.

"Zar, I don't think any of the women can go home." I hate to verbalize this fact out loud, but it has to be discussed. "Some of us might be pregnant. Humans are…"

I've told Zar all the good things about Earth. I hate to admit how judgmental and bloodthirsty some of us can be. "Humans can be tribal. We choose sides and don't like or trust people who are other than ourselves. If we came home with hybrid babies… we'd be targets for people who hate. And there are a lot of haters in the world."

"The babies wouldn't be safe?"

"None of us would be safe." I shake my head sadly.

His shoulders tighten and pull back. He's gone into protective mode even though we're millions of miles from Earth.

"And even without babies, if anyone on Earth found out aliens are real, it would cause pandemonium. Or, more likely, they would accuse us of being insane and lock us up forever. I don't think any of us can ever go home."

The import of what I just said hits me—I feel gut-punched. Never is a long time. Never going home means no parents, no sisters, no Midnight the cat. No blue skies or my old Corolla or even my shitty job… none of it. Ever. I blink back hot tears.

We finally realize it's been a long day. Between the gladiatorial competition, the world-class marathon sex, and the mental gymnastics of planning for any and every eventuality of overthrowing this spaceship, we're tired. The Urluts' morning wake-up call will come all too quickly.

Zar

At the Urluts' command, Anya and I have that quiet intimate sex where we stare into each other's eyes while we mate. It's not the panting, hot, furious sex of yesterday where we couldn't couple fast enough. It's slow and breathtakingly intense and feels like there are two bodies and only one soul. Anya might not agree, but I like this even better than the other. It connects me to another living being in a way that even intense physical satisfaction cannot.

It doesn't surprise me when I realize I would die for her. Easily. Almost happily. In a span of only a few days, I've discovered I have a reason for living, and that reason is Anya. She could casually ask me to walk into hell for her and I would, without question.

Perhaps Shadow is right when he says I've lost my mind.

I begrudgingly agree with Anya when she reminds me today cannot be the day to overthrow the enemy. We have to make sure "all systems are go," as she says. We haven't tested Shadow and Tyree's link from the bridge to the *ludus*. It would be foolhardy to fight today without knowing if that communication will work.

This angers me. I'm ready to fight. Win or lose, I hate the waiting. Perhaps I wasn't born to be the general who orches-trates the fight. I was born to be the one who rushes into battle and counts the bodies of those I've slain.

Anya

Dr. Drayke tries as usual to keep the exam quick and all business. I try to pump him for information. Today is some-what different, however, because I'm not inquiring about the workings of the ship or trying to figure out why he's here. I'm trying to determine what he'll do when the shit hits the fan tomorrow.

With my feet planted firmly on the floor, I begin. "Have you ever thought about leaving the ship? Maybe finding a passenger vessel at the next stop and deserting?"

His deep-set blue eyes take my full measure. His entire demeanor changes, his muscles tightening, as he assesses me warily. "Why do you ask that, Miss Anya?"

"Well," I hedge, "you just seem so miserable here. I know you don't feel right doing... what you do. How bad would it be to just slip away and create a new life? They probably need doctors all over the galaxy."

"Just slip away, huh? My contract isn't with the Urluts or the captain of this ship. My contract is officially with the Trans-Galaxy Shipping and Transport Agency. It sounded legitimate enough when I signed it. It was only after the documents were completed that I learned Trans-Galaxy was just one of many front organizations for the MarZan cartel."

He leans his jumpsuited hip against the exam table and crosses his arms over his chest.

"They are one of the most powerful, cutthroat, vindictive confederations out there. If I just 'slip away' as you suggest, they will hunt me down and find me wherever I am in the galaxy. Yes, they will kill me, but that will be the easy and merciful part of what they will do to me. I won't even mention some of the stories I've heard." He breathes deeply and shakes his head ruefully.

"And that doesn't even address what they will first do to my family. No, no matter how horrible my life is, I will ride out my contract."

His eyes focus on the wall above my right shoulder.

"I try to help the people I treat. Above all, I'm a healer. I've been nothing but kind to all of you females. I've patched up some of the gladiators as well, always attempting to be compassionate and caring. I sometimes even convince the captain to provide extra rations or other enhancements to the captives' lives.

"I'm staying, Anya. It is hell for me, but I can see no options."

I'm partly processing his words and what they mean to him, but mostly focused on the fact that even if we win this battle, we're going to be hunted down by one of the most dangerous smuggling cartels in the galaxy.

I leave the exam knowing where Dr. Drayke's allegiances lie. "Above all do no harm," may be an Earth saying, but this male would never fight against us, would never harm us. If he's smart, he'll lock himself in medbay tomorrow and wait for the shooting to end.

Tyree

I wait for a quiet moment on the bridge, then let the tentacles of my mind reach through the ship. I'm still just learning how to make this happen. Even as I do it, I'm not sure if I find Shadow by mentally tracing my steps through the ship to the *ludus*, or if I find him by seeking his unique mental signature. Perhaps a little of both.

At any rate, it's fairly easy to lock onto him and begin a conversation. *Shadow, Shadow, Shadow,* I call. I feel his angry awareness on me almost immediately.

You're interrupting my sparring, he accuses.

We need to do this, asshole. Whoops, that isn't my style at all. I'm not sure where that came from.

Well, you contacted me and I responded, what else do you need to know?

I terminate our connection. How can one male be such an annoying prick? Oh well, mission accomplished. I believe this is the last piece we needed to tie down to make certain we can fight the crew. I hope we can get this over with tomorrow. It's getting harder to be in the same quarters with the captain. I hate him more with each passing day.

Chapter Fourteen

ANYA

Zar can read my glum mood as soon as the Urluts push him into our cell. When I explain what we'll be up against if we win and take over the ship, he doesn't seem scared, he just appears thoughtful.

"This doesn't worry you?" I'm pacing the tiny cell, my mind jumping from one obstacle to another. "It overwhelms me."

"In my life, I've found there is always one bad thing after another, Anya. How could you expect anything better?"

For the millionth time since my abduction, I realize my life on Earth, as shitty as I sometimes thought it was, was really freaking easy. In my old life, did I actually let bad hair days, running out of gas, or being ghosted by a mediocre date ruin my day? I wish I could take all that back. Now I know what a bad day *really* is.

"So, we just go from one crisis to the next? Just like that? We just learn to take it?" My voice has risen and a bystander might label the tone "hysterical."

Zar's lips compress. I think he might be figuring out how to "manage" me. Fuck him, I hate being "managed" when I'm losing control.

"Yes, Anya. Life is a series of events that often go from one dilemma to another. But it's the *middle* that's important. It's what's between the crises that's so vital. Look at what's happening here." He gestures at the two of us.

"What's happening between you and me, Anya. The sweet perfection of *this*. The miracle of finding each other in the midst of the crazy and the pain and the abuse. We've found each other. *That* is what makes life worth living."

He's piercing me with his warm golden gaze. My heart clenches at the truth of what he said. Life is *not* just a bowl of cherries. As someone once said, it's mostly pits. But when you find that one delicious dark cherry that bursts with sweetness in your mouth, you can savor it and enjoy it all the more.

I didn't ask to be here. I didn't ask to be on this ship, in a cell, away from home. But here I am, and I found my amazing lion guy, and I love him. We'll fight this fight, and we will win. And then we'll fight the next and the next. Whatever they throw at us, we won't give up. But we'll have each other, and Zar's right, that's what makes life worth living.

I throw myself into his arms, practically demanding his embrace. This male, with no formal education of any kind, is the smartest person I know. And patient. He's so patient with me. I press my cheek to his soft-as-velvet pec and inhale the clean scent of him. I love the strong muscles under my fingertips, everywhere my hands roam.

My emotions are scrambled. So much fear, anger, and frustration are swirling around me in a jumbled mess. But as I sort through all those feelings, I find I can relegate them to just background noise and focus on what I want. And what I want to focus on? Love. I choose love.

Zar

I've always been taught that sex before a fight drains your power. Anya tells me I'm crazy, that on her planet that's been disproven. She's pretty persuasive, especially after she adds kisses and caresses to the debate, but I don't want to lose strength before tomorrow's battle. She's cute when she pouts, but then backs off and seems content to just rest in my arms.

Lying in bed, she peppers me with questions about tomorrow. I reassure her that every male is aware of the plan. I've shared every detail with Axxios and Shadow, and they made sure all the others are in agreement.

It was harder for me to catch Doctoré alone due to all his duties as our trainer, and that the guards watch him so closely. He was an honored champion in the arena for many *annums.* When he was in his prime, he was far more skilled than I.

He keeps his calm and does his job, but underneath his tranquil exterior, he seethes with anger. Rumor has it his owner cheated him out of buying his freedom, then sold him to an even harsher master. He'll fight well for our cause.

Me, I've always known I would never have freedom. I imagine it's much easier to tolerate living in slavery than to believe you might one day be free and then have that snatched from you.

It strikes me briefly that I might have my freedom by tomorrow evening, then I push that thought into the far recesses of my mind.

Don't dream too big. I learned that young. I learned that with my friend Pallatin. Right now, I only have one thing to hold onto. That is my little Anya. I have this magic with Anya. Even if I die tomorrow, I had these days with her and will die happy. If I perish during this rebellion, in my heart I know I will die a free male and not a slave, and that is good and right and just.

Anya is facing me, her head on my outstretched bicep. I stroke her soft hair with my fingertips, then use my claws as a comb, trying to reassure her with my touch. Her nervous thoughts flick from one worry to another as she voices them out loud. I must admit, my mind is full of worries too. The crew outguns us. We're not sure we can turn off the collars.

There are so many possible pitfalls. Everyone in this cell block knows we might not live to see another day.

I hadn't wanted to bring this up to Anya. I hadn't wanted her to worry, or to grasp too clearly that one or both of us might die tomorrow. But she's already terrified.

"Anya, I want you to promise me something."

"What?" Her tone is immediately sober. It's obvious I want to have a serious talk.

I place my palm on her belly. We've barely discussed the possibility that she might be carrying my young. Piercing her with my gaze, I tell her, "If we succeed in gaining our freedom but I die tomorrow—" She interrupts me, shushing me to get me to change the subject. I place a finger on her lips and shake my head. I have to say this. She must listen. She understands, takes a measured breath, and nods her head to signal she's ready to hear what I have to say.

"If I die tomorrow, if you live and have our young, I want you to tell him or her two things."

Her eyes luminous with unshed tears, she listens intently with her lips clamped shut.

"I want you to explain that I saved their mother from slavery."

Anya looks at me tenderly, stroking my arm. "If I carry your young, I will tell him or her about their father's finest hour. But you'll be there with me, to correct the story and make sure I'm getting all the details right."

I don't have the heart to force her to accept that I might die tomorrow. We both know the reality here.

"And what is the second thing you want me to tell?"

I pierce her with the tenderest gaze. A flood of loving warmth gushes through every fiber of my being. I want her to remember this moment forever. "Tell our young how much their father loved their mother."

Her tears spill freely now, and she nestles against me. She hugs me so tightly there is no air between our bodies. She kisses me wildly—cheeks, eyes, forehead, neck, anywhere her lips can reach.

Both of us are lying on our sides in a tight embrace. My palm slides down her neck, along her spine, to her sweetly rounded bottom. Then back up to her neck and down again. She's focused on my hand, on this intimate connection. My fingers roam lower, stroking the globes of her ass, squeezing a bit. I'm certain I have her full attention.

She puts up no resistance when I slip her pants off.

"I thought we weren't...?"

"*We* aren't, Little Anya," I say as I slip one finger down her bottom from behind, between her cheeks to the waiting folds of her sex.

"Mmmm..." She lifts one leg and cocks it, resting her knee on my leg to open herself to my hand, giving me better access.

My finger presses from behind through her folds. She's wet for me, as she always seems to be. I dip my finger into her core and she involuntarily sucks in a breath and clenches with pleasure, then opens for me again. My finger now drenched in her juices, I reach forward to swirl it around her little button of pleasure, then pull back to dip my finger in her wetness again.

Her breathing has changed completely from a soft, calm rhythm to open-mouthed pants. My finger continues to alternate between swirling around her clit to penetration and back again. At first just the tip of my finger, now all the way in to the hilt. Her hips are bucking, and she's trying to stifle the moans erupting from the back of her throat.

She flips onto her back, her knees splayed in open invitation. I know what she wants—more pressure, more penetration, but I want to ramp her up even higher. Under the blanket, I kneel between her legs to get better range of motion and begin a steady rhythm of thrusts. After a moment of this, I press into her with two fingers. A soft murmur escapes her lips even as her hips lift to meet me more insistently.

"Please," it's a breathy plea.

I move down and put my knees on the floor at the foot of the bed. Grabbing her ankles, I pull her lower. Now she's in the perfect position for my mouth, her heels on the edge of the bed, her knees open to me, still under the blanket for some measure of privacy.

Two fingers in her warm core, I lap at her little button. She hisses in pleasure. I was afraid the burrs on my tongue would hurt her tender parts, but she seems on fire and isn't complaining.

Her fingers alternate between combing through my mane and pressing my head down harder on her sensitive bud. I glance up to see her head thrown back in ecstasy. No, I don't think my abrasive tongue is causing any pain.

"Zar." It's part request, part insistence. I can tell she's close. I press harder with my tongue at the same moment I add a third finger to penetrate deeply into her drenched channel.

"Yesss," she hisses, trying to be quiet. Her internal muscles clamp around my fingers as her entire body responds in waves of pleasure. It seems to go on forever, these deep spasms of ecstasy. I bask in the joy of giving her so much bliss. It feels so good to attend to my female like this.

"So beautiful," I praise. This seems to help her wring a few more moments of ecstasy out of our mating.

After a moment's recovery time, she grabs me and pulls me up until we're both lying properly on the bed again.

"That was amazing. Toe-curling," she says.

Yes, indeed.

"What about you, Zar?"

"Keeping the fluids in, Anya. It keeps a warrior strong. I want to be strong to fight for you tomorrow."

Chapter Fifteen

ZAR

I know I should focus on today's fight, but I woke up early and couldn't sleep. It seems so unfair that something wonderful drops into my life and in only a few short days I might lose it again. I won't concentrate on that. She's in my arms now and I want to take advantage of it.

I extend my claws and gently scratch her naked back. I'm not sure she will like it.

"For the love of God, what are you doing?"

I immediately retract my claws and lift my hand off her as if it were on fire.

"Don't stop! Are those your claws?"

I don't even answer, I just return to softly scratching up and down her back.

"That's about the sexiest thing I've ever experienced. Why didn't you tell me you had that superpower before? Do. Not. Stop." She lies fully on her front so I have better access to all of her backside.

I think she's purring.

My hand reaches lower, on her ass.

"Zar, never ever stop. That is so terrific."

I experiment, pressing the tiniest bit harder. She sucks in a sharp breath. Yes, she likes that, too. Then I move up to her scalp.

"Zar, that's divine. It's a secret weapon. No female in the galaxy could resist this."

Another purr.

I realize it's not her who is purring. That purr is coming from me. I didn't know I could produce that sound.

"Are you purring?"

"I guess I am. I've never done it before. What would cause such a thing?"

"Back on Earth," she pauses, then admonishes, "don't stop!" when I slow down. "Back on Earth, the animals that remind me of you, well, not the lions, but the smaller cat-like animals, purr when they're relaxed and happy."

"I'm certainly not relaxed with the most important battle of my life about to happen. But Anya, I *am* happy. No matter what happens today, know you've made me happy."

Anya

The Urluts order us to "complete the act" on cue. I know Zar doesn't want to lose any precious bodily fluids, but I don't want to lose my head either, so we comply.

Frankly, it's surreal. Neither of us addresses it, but I'm sure both of us are thinking this could be the last time we see each other. One or both of us could die today. Our lovemaking is just that—making love. It's so tender, so intimate, so connected. There is absolutely nothing carnal about what we are doing in this bed, under these covers. We are tying our souls in an inextricable knot.

When the door to the cell block clangs open, we're both dressed and ready to go. Before the guards approach our cell, he touches my lips in the sweetest kiss imaginable. He softly pounds his fist against his chest and bows his head in the way gladiators honor each other.

"I will see you later today," he says with certainty. I know he's trying to calm me.

"Yes. When we see each other later, we will be free," I whisper with a conviction I don't fully believe.

Zar

My shoulders sag a bit as the loud metal doors clang behind me. I didn't want Anya to worry about me any more than she has to, but this is not going to be the easy battle I've been all but promising. It will be seasoned warrior against seasoned warrior. We gladiators have experience and the will to win. However much we want to be free, and no matter how great our skill, as soon as we attack the Urluts they'll go into high gear to protect themselves. And they have superior weapons.

When it is kill or be killed, it tends to motivate you. Our enemy is not going to lie down and hand over their weapons. I know full well, this is going to be a tough battle.

I can feel the other males' tension and excitement. We're all standing taller, walking faster, more alert, more on edge. I'm surprised the Urluts don't figure out something is up. There is a palpable change in us today.

The plan is for me and whoever I'm paired with to attack first. It's going to depend on where we're placed in the *ludus* and who is guarding whom. Helix and Bellarn are guarding us, which is to our great good fortune. Helix was injured just a few days ago in the Marauder attack—he will not be at full fighting strength.

They order Shadow and me to grapple, meaning we'll have no weapons at our disposal, not even those pitiful wooden swords. Fate goes in our direction one moment, then disappears just as quickly.

"We can do this even without weapons," I tell Shadow. "I'll take Bellarn, you take Helix."

"I'll take Bellarn," Shadow asserts, "you take Helix."

I realize what we're doing. We're each trying to give the other the easiest opponent. "My claws and fangs are stronger weapons than your bionic arm," I argue.

"Perhaps, my brother, but you have something to live for. I do not."

My head pops back in surprise. Shadow has never been particularly nice before, not to me, not to anyone. Not only did he call me "brother," but he's willing to sacrifice his life for mine. I raise my eyebrow in question.

"Your female," he explains. "You have your female to live for. Let me take the biggest risk."

It's a generous offer, but I'm not comfortable with it. However, all Shadow has now is his honor and dignity. To take that away from him, possibly on the eve of his death, is not an option.

I clasp his arm and nod. "I shall not forget this."

"I'll say *'drack'* loudly when Tyree tells me the collars are off," Shadow murmurs.

"Don't forget, we don't know how long Tyree can keep the captain from turning them back on again. We must move fast."

We grapple, going through the motions with each other, both fully focused on the two Urluts in our peripheral vision. The two soon become bored with our lackluster performance and relax their grip on their weapons. We're still waiting for word from Tyree. By the harsh look on Shadow's face, I know she's given the all-clear even before he yells *"drack."*

The Urluts have dropped their guard completely as they argue good-naturedly about a gambling game they played in their quarters last night.

Shadow and I catch each other's glances and charge the guards at the same moment. We have only a *modicum* before they notice we're moving on them. Helix wastes no time grabbing his wrist control for our collars as he shouts, "Down on your knees, hands behind your heads you filthy assholes."

I'm upon him before he fully realizes the collar controllers aren't working. I'd already seen that he favored his right side due to his injuries. It's the work of a moment to grab his wrist and pull him toward me, exactly the opposite of what he'd been expecting.

He totters, off-balance, and I grab the shock baton he'd already pulled from his belt. I thrust the butt end of the baton into his midsection with all my might, then flip my grip and press the shock control as I jab the weapon into the same spot.

The Urlut shrieks in pain and doubles over, clutching his stomach. I hope I hit him directly in his previous wound. While he's gasping for breath, I throw the baton to the side, knowing one of my brothers will have it in hand before it hits the ground.

I've easily disabled the male. He's on his knees, gasping in agony. I could tie him up and somehow get him to a cell. I know this wasn't the plan. All Urluts were to be eliminated, but it seems wrong to kill a male who I've already overpowered.

As I move to grab his hands to tie them behind his back, Helix fumbles desperately, trying to aim his laser at me. The time for tying and capturing is over. I have to end him. I fall with all my weight upon my knee which is resting on his chest. At the same time, I power my elbow into his collarbone. The force cracks his collarbone with an explosive sound, and his yowl of pain is earsplitting. Grabbing his head, I give it a swift twist until it gives a brittle snap as he loses all muscle tone and falls heavily to the floor. Unquestionably dead. I glance around and see Shadow has already dispatched Bellarn.

All ten of us stand stock still. The room is silent except for our heavy breathing. We're listening for shouts, the alert klaxons, the sounds of males rushing to the *ludus*—nothing. I've grabbed Helix's laser, Shadow has Bellarn's. We have two laser guns, two laser rifles, and two laser batons. We distribute among us six laser weapons of varying power strengths.

We're ready to start a slave revolution.

Axxios has already grabbed the keycards off Bellarn's belt and is rummaging in the weapons room. In a moment, all of us have a weapon, albeit some are only wood. A few have grabbed wooden shields—I refuse one, thinking it will only slow me down.

"Shadow, Steele, and I at the tip of the spear," I pronounce. "Doctoré, Stryker and Dax at the rear. We keep in tight formation, heading straight for the bridge. I believe the other Urlut is in his quarters, so be aware he may come at our flanks or rear. The quicker we get to the bridge, the better. Tyree can't keep the collars disabled for long. As soon as we have them at bay, the three of you rear guard must go room to room throughout the ship, subduing any others."

I remember Anya's final words to me as I left the cell this morning, "Protect the doctor."

"We'll need the medic," I tell the men forcefully. "Keep him alive unless he fights."

We move swiftly through the hallways in tight formation as if we've trained for this our entire lives. In a way, I guess we have.

Because of the Marauder attack, we know the layout of the ship and the way to the bridge. We move swift and sure in that direction.

"Tyree says she's losing control," Shadow announces. "She says she can't keep the collars disabled much longer."

"*Drack*!"

We quicken our pace, but I'm fearful of making too much noise.

One of the mechanics is absentmindedly wandering toward a storage area when he looks up from the portable vid he's engrossed in, sees a well-armed and deadly contingent of gladiators bearing down on him, and runs toward the nearest alarm button. He manages to press it before Steele nearly cuts him in half with a burst of laser fire.

The red lights now flashing, klaxons screaming, we have no reason for stealth. We burst into a run, heading straight for the bridge. When we round the corner, the doors are closing. Steele takes quick aim and blasts the doors with continuous fire until he disables the left one, leaving it yawning open at an odd angle.

We barge in, ten armed and angry career warriors. The captain is in his chair, surprise written on his face, eyes wide in fear. Four gladiators point laser weapons directly at his chest and he raises his arms in total surrender.

The first mate is at a computer station, his fingers flying on his keyboard. I turn my weapon and full attention to him.

"Stand down," I order. When he doesn't immediately comply, I focus my weapon on his chest. "Stop!"

He continues to type, probably sending a request for help along with our coordinates. I shoot him, and he falls over his keyboard, bleeding from a gaping chest wound.

"Anyone know computers? Any way to terminate his last communication?" Before the words are out of my mouth,

Axxios is pushing the first mate's lifeless body to the floor, commandeering the computer station and typing frantically.

I give another visual sweep of the small bridge to ensure there's no one else to contend with. First mate down, captain well under control. I walk around and find little Tyree in the kneehole of one of the workstations. I reach in and help her out. She looks awful. More than scared, her color is off and her face looks misshapen, almost as if she's been slapped or punched.

"I'm fine," she tells me, almost as if she can read my mind. Perhaps she can.

"Steele, Dax, stay here while we secure the rest of the ship. Axxios, can you keep working on that and take the helm if need be?"

He nods, completely preoccupied with the computer.

Theos has already checked the captain for arms, grabbed the first mate's weapon, and is ready to roll.

"Let's go room to room. There's one more Urlut, two service staff, and a mechanic. We need to find the doctor and keep him safe. When everyone is rounded up, we'll take the prisoners to lockup and free the females."

Although most of our enemy is dead, there is still the possibility of attack by the remaining crew. My heart is pounding against my breastbone with worry. Not for me, though. What if one of the crew knew our weakness and is holding the females hostage? I need to dispatch the remaining males and make sure Anya is safe and in my arms again.

Anya

Well crap. I'd believed we had thought this through completely a thousand times, but we didn't take the timing fully into account. Tyree just told me the collars are deactivated. Now every step I take on my way to medbay I'm waiting for shouting, laser fire, or klaxons. I hope I get there in one piece.

At this point, the safest thing for both myself and Dr. Drayke is for us to stay together until this thing is over. I'll just have to stall during the exam, which shouldn't alert him since I do it every day anyway.

Just as the Urlut drops me at the exam room the alarms erupt. Not the brightest bulb in the string, he looks confused for a moment as he considers whether he should stay here or go find where the trouble is. He makes his decision, pushes me into the room with the doctor, and closes the door. Did he just lock us in together?

Dr. Drayke looks panicked. "Another Marauder attack?" he wonders out loud.

I consider spilling the beans, but if this insurrection goes south, I don't want him to know anything. He can claim innocence and stay alive.

My heart clenches in terror. The next hour will probably be the most important—and dangerous—in my life.

Chapter Sixteen

Zar

We swiftly explore every hallway, bathroom, and closet. Two uniformed workers who must be cleaning or cooking crew are already on their knees, facing the wall, hands behind their heads when we barge into their cabin. It wouldn't be honorable to kill them. We tie their hands behind their backs and march them with us as we continue our search.

The remaining Urlut tries to sneak up behind us. It's a ridiculous attempt, considering we hear his lumbering steps long before we see him. He's dead from a laser blast before he topples to the floor.

If Tyree's intel was correct, other than the doctor, there is one more crew member, a mechanic. We're moving fast toward the engine room, investigating nooks and crannies along the way.

We hit the medbay and find a locked inner door. Axxios's stolen passcard gives us quick access. Now we'll see if Anya's doctor is going to fight us or not. We barge into the little exam room, guns drawn and ready to end him if need be. We find not only the doc but my sweet Anya. Both look wide-eyed and scared to death. He swiftly raises his blue hands in surrender.

My males handle the medic while I pull Anya into my arms. After a brief hug, I step away, my hands on her shoulders, as I inspect her. She looks unharmed, just scared. Grabbing me, she squeezes tight. "I was so worried about you."

"And I you." My chest clenches with emotion, then expands with relief. I'm so glad she's safe and in my arms. I can't wait to finish the sweep of the ship, lock up the enemy, and figure out what quadrant to speed off to.

Now that I have my precious Anya in tow, I slow our pace a bit as we finish our search. We can't be too careful. All we have is the engine room and our first recon will be complete.

I open the engine room door, leaving Anya in the hall with Stryker, Theos, the doc, and the two captives. Shadow and I enter the engine room, guns drawn. I'm on full alert. We're missing a mechanic, and it doesn't make sense for him to be anywhere but here.

I've never been in an engine room and don't know what to expect. It's dirty and cluttered, with tools scattered on the floor. Shadow moves left, I move right. This place is so messy, with so much machinery, there are all sorts of places to hide. There's literally a wall of food ration boxes cocked at a random angle near what appears to be a storage room. I vaguely wonder if the mechs are running a black-market food sales operation under the captain's nose.

There's a rustling noise behind the wall of boxes. Before I can approach, Shadow charges from my left, running point. I think it's another misguided attempt to protect me.

We both advance to the far right edge when the wall of boxes falls toward us. Shadow takes the brunt of the collapse and is swiftly buried beneath a dozen large, heavy cartons.

Jumping back, I avoid them, but before I can check on him, a male launches at me, swinging a large tool at my head. I duck, feeling the air swish near my cheek. Instinctively, I thrust my weapon, aiming for his heart, only to realize I hold a gun in my hand, not my sword. The male takes the blow to his shoulder, twisting to avoid much of the impact, then thrusts forward with his right hand.

Sharp pain slices into my abdomen, causing me to roar in pain and fury. Grabbing his wrist as he swings backhanded with the tool, I prevent the second attempted blow to my head, but as he avoids my grip, he pushes harder on whatever is lodged in my gut.

I fire my laser into his chest, causing him to drop like a stone, pulling the weapon from my abdomen in his still-tight grip.

Bright red blood gushes from my wound. Dropping my gun, I press both hands to the hole. My physical agony is second to my outrage that an untrained mechanic surprised two seasoned gladiators and managed to inflict a wound that, judging from the amount of blood flowing from between my fingers, could be fatal.

Dropping to my knees as I become lightheaded, numbness renders my legs useless. Darkness descends as I crash to my side.

Anya. It is so unfair to leave her now. I've just found her. Pain lances my heart, feeling a hundred times worse than the stab to my abdomen. This time, I'm too weak to allow the roar of loss and grief that wants to erupt from my chest. At least she's now free.

"Zar!" Shadow's yell sounds like it's coming from across the galaxy. Then, nothing.

Anya

I'd expected laser fire to erupt from the engine room, assuming the mech was hiding there. I did not expect to hear a crash, or the gut-wrenching sound of my lion-man roaring in agony. Stryker and Theos have to physically prevent me from running in, although I don't know what I could do to help.

Shadow shouts, "Zar!" his voice laced with shock and fury. "Enemy dead. Zar's down," he shouts, each word a staccato stab to my chest. By the time the males release me, Dr. Drayke is already halfway through the doorway, hurrying to assess the situation.

Drayke is kneeling next to Zar's crumpled and bloody body which is lying next to a pile of boxes. The mechanic with a black hole in his chest is sprawled on top of them, still holding a bloody tool that looks like a ten-inch screwdriver in one hand and an enormous pipe wrench in the other.

"No!" I cry, then shove my knuckles against my lips. My chest feels tight and heavy, tears well in my eyes. I don't want to distract even one iota from the doctor's concentration. I bite back my urge to ask if Zar will be okay. There's no way the doctor could know anything at this point. I'm impotent, just a nuisance.

Kneeling at Zar's side, I try to stay out of the doctor's way. Stroking Zar's hand, I murmur nonsense. What do you say when you see your male gravely injured only inches from you? This is so real and yet it's as if I'm seeing it from a distance.

Out of the edge of my awareness, I notice Theos heading toward medbay while Stryker hustles the prisoners to the cell block to secure them and check on the other women. I'm too busy paying attention to Zar's blood-soaked chest as it weakly rises and falls.

It seems hours before Theos returns, running at full speed, one hand on the hover gurney beside him. The males pick Zar up and set him on it without him making a sound. He's unconscious—no muscle tone, head lolled to the side, lips drooping and fangs gleaming in the dim light. And blood. So much blood. A crazy part of my brain tells me Zar is dead, but the sane part of me insists they wouldn't be doing this if he were no longer alive.

I trail behind as Shadow speeds the gurney to medbay with Dr. Drayke running beside, pressing his hands over the wound that is still gushing blood. Before Shadow even locks the legs in place in the operating room, Drayke tells Theos to hold pressure on the wound, then the blue doctor shifts into overdrive as the lights and screen over the table flick on. He orders the medbot to administer IV fluids, compatible blood, and a clotting agent while he intently examines the medical information streaming in on a nearby screen. His fingers fly over the screen as his eyes scan the results.

Standing at the head of the gurney, I stay as out of the way as possible while the medbot starts the infusion of blood into one of Zar's arms and the bag of clear fluid into the other. I stroke Zar's immobile face. My God, I feel half-dead myself. This can't be happening.

If even a tiny part of me had still wondered if I loved Zar, there is no doubt now. If I just kind of liked this guy because we were in a dangerous situation together, my heart wouldn't feel as if it had been plucked, still beating, out of my chest. It's love all right, and with him lying so close to death on that gurney, it's the downside of love for sure.

What if he dies? Did I tell him I loved him? What if I never talk to him—never see that rare, beautiful smile beam at me again?

I can't bear what I'm feeling. I shrink back into myself and put these worries and thoughts out of my head. Witnessing it as if through a fog—my vision is blurry. I hear the doctor's staccato commands as though I'm underwater.

Observing every movement the doctor makes, I watch as the medbot performs what looks like intricate surgery on the wound in Zar's abdomen. The doctor's face is tense as he observes the procedure on the screen, then announces, "Perforated bowel and a tear in the abdominal aorta. He's lucky the weapon was sharp on the end and not along the edges like a knife. That damage would have been irreparable."

Irreparable. The word echoes in my mind, reverberating louder and louder until it consumes my thoughts. Shaking my head, I bring myself to the present and try to pay attention.

"Another couple of *minimas* and he would have bled out. The damage to the bowel and the open artery has created the worst-case scenario. I'm programming the medbot to add antibiotics to the IV fluid and flush the abdomen with an antibiotic solution. "

I clamp my teeth shut, but no amount of pressure keeps my grief from spilling out. Tears are raining down my face. I experience the unbearable pain of hearing that the man I love might not make it.

Hearing a commotion, I look up to see what must be all the males and women in the hall outside the medbay door.

"Is he going to be alright?" A female voice asks.

Theos had removed his hands from Zar's abdomen as the medbot took over. The bright red blood still clinging to his milk-white hands is a shocking contrast.

Despite his bloody appearance and his attempt to calm the people in the hallway, his voice is tight as he says, "Zar is alive. Dr. Drayke is doing everything possible. Let's leave them. There is nothing any of us can do to help here. We all probably need some food."

"I'm a chef," Maddie says. "I'll produce something edible in the time it takes for everyone to..." she gives a pointed look to Theos's hands, "clean up."

Shadow pulls a wheeled stool behind me and gently presses my shoulders so I'm sitting. I never take my hands off Zar's face and mane as I stroke him, hoping my fingers communicate to him in a way words can't.

Part of my brain acknowledges Shadow's considerate gesture, which is a shock considering how he treats Grace. All I can do is give him a quick glance and a nod of appreciation. Even more surprising, he nods back, his features taut and worried despite the robotic eye. He leaves the medbay to the three of us.

"Nothing to do but wait," Dr. Drayke announces. "We've done everything we can do. The medbot patched things up. I'm replacing lost blood."

He pushes bloodied gauze out of my line of sight, then continues, "The perforated bowel means there are nasty bacteria everywhere in his internal cavity. This has led to infection or sepsis, especially because the germs infiltrated his blood through the damaged abdominal aorta, which is the large blood vessel traveling from the heart to the lower body. If this had happened any farther from an operating room, he'd already be dead. If the infection overwhelms his heart or brain..." He sees me blanch. "But he has a chance, Anya. He's strong and healthy. He has a chance."

Drayke lifts the hover gurney and moves Zar from the operating room, still hooked up to the IV, into one of the smaller exam rooms. After lowering the hover to convert into a bed, he covers Zar with a warming blanket and leaves us alone.

Now I allow myself to fully experience the grief and fear I've been trying to control. My hands are shaking so badly I press them between my thighs to settle down. I can't see Zar through my watery eyes. I wish I could just disappear.

I love this guy. He's so medically compromised I don't know if he'll live or die.

I've seen enough TV medical shows to know that comatose people are supposed to be able to hear their loved ones talk. So, by God, I'm going to keep up a steady stream of chatter. Zar is going to know I'm here and how much I love his beautiful, whiskered face.

Chapter Seventeen

Anya

It's been touch and go with Zar for two days. I've barely left his side. I've been eating bars when ordered by the doc, and even had some soup he had delivered to me. Yippee, the first food other than bars (and that fantastic Joyous Jane knockoff) I've had in... I have no idea how many days it's been since I was kidnapped from Earth.

I've taken a shower every day and Grace, bless her heart, brought me some actual clothes that were found in the laundry area. I never thought I'd be so thrilled to be wearing blue coveralls, but I am.

Grace tells me Axxios, our golden pilot, had to make some executive decisions about where we're going. We're bound toward planet Numa in some star system I can't remember. Why I would care is beyond me. What difference does it make?

We know we're probably being chased. After all, we've absconded with a well-equipped ship and a bunch of expensive livestock—namely us. The Trans-Galaxy consortium aka the MarZan Cartel is probably plenty pissed. We're going to have to pay heavily to change our ship's name, vehicle ident numbers, and hailing signal.

I've only half listened to all of this because I'm not leaving this room until Zar is better. So I have no say in any of the decisions. Do I sound like a junior high school girl if I say I don't particularly care where we go or what happens if Zar isn't with me? I know I'm a strong, capable woman who used to be in charge of her own life, but I'm bonded to my lion guy and can't imagine life without him.

Dr. Drayke says he still doesn't know if Zar will regain consciousness, but it's a good sign he's still with us. Well, yeah, that's ridiculously obvious.

The medbot has done everything it can, as has the doctor himself. He says all we can do is keep pumping him full of IV antibiotics, fluids, and nutrients and wait. He explained the formula he's administering is 100% absorbed by the body, thus bypassing the need to eliminate waste.

I'm sitting at Zar's side, my head resting near his heart, and dozing on and off even though it's daytime. It's kind of boring just sitting here with no one to talk to. I have to say, with access to the broadcasts from most of the known planets in the universe, I still think Netflix has better programming. There's not one thing on the portable vid they gave me that's worth watching.

I must be fast asleep when Zar's breathing changes. Startling awake, I sit up quickly to see how he's doing. Those gorgeous, golden cat's eyes are looking straight at me. He gives me a weak smile, but it *is* a smile.

"Zar, you're awake!" Duh, but I'm almost speechless knowing he's back among the living.

"Anya," is all he can croak out through a scratchy voice.

I raise the head of the bed and scramble to get him some water as I just keep repeating how worried I was and how much I love him. He's weak as a kitten and can hardly raise his hand to grab the glass, but there's a little sparkle in his eyes as he looks at me.

Better hydrated now, he says, "I love you, too," and drifts back to sleep.

OVER THE NEXT DAY, he's been waking regularly and has nibbled on a nutrition bar. Axxios came to visit and helped Zar shower. He's still far too weak to stand by himself.

Now Zar is clean, looking slightly refreshed, and sitting up in bed. Axxios uses a small tool to remove our collars. I've been so preoccupied, I didn't even give it a thought, but when it comes off in the pilot's hand, I sigh in relief.

"As God is my witness," I say, "I will never wear one of those things again."

"Aye," Zar says, looking at the two collars in Axxios's hand in disgust.

The pilot sits down with both of us to give us an update. This is the first time I've heard anything other than secondhand news from Grace or the doc.

"It's been a shitshow," Axxios begins, then scrubs his hand over his face. "I won't go into every detail, suffice it to say we've been patching problems since I sat down at the controls four days ago. We aren't being pursued now as best we can tell, but it's only a matter of time until MarZan comes looking for their property, and they are going to be pissed.

"We're going to planet Numa, several days from here. It's at the ass-end of the universe and a far grittier place even than Hyperion. There's a lot we'll need to do, including changing the name and call number of this ship, as well as paying off authorities so we can hide there for a while.

"Savannah, the female who roomed with Theos, was a mechanic on the primitive aircraft on her planet. She was in Earth's military. She's located a tracking device, shimmied into a crawl space in the engine room, and disabled it. A brilliant move. It will take the cartel a while longer to find us without that signal broadcasting our location.

"There are a lot of gladiator fights on Numa with little to no Federation presence. I think that's the only way we can pick up some quick credits to pay for the work and supplies we're going to need. Every gladiator on board is volunteering for that duty. It will be the first time any of us have fought as free males. Making our own choice to fight is sweet indeed."

"Winning will be even sweeter," Zar interjects. "Make sure you choose our best to fight. We'll need the credits."

"Absolutely. We're on top of that. On a different note, we all agree, including the women, that even if we could make our way back to their home planet, it is not an option. Someone would inevitably talk, and the shitstorm it would produce would make life intolerable for them all. A few of them are convinced they'd be painfully vivisected and studied."

I feel a pang of sadness at the finality of his pronouncement, even though I've had this same thought for days. It's still depressing to know I'll never go home again.

"We've got some decisions to make," Axxios continues. "We have three captives: the captain and two cleaning crew. The moment we let them go, they'll be contacting MarZan or the authorities, or both. We'd better be *dracki*ng sure we have everything in order before we cut them loose. We could... dispose of them otherwise if necessary. It's still an option."

"I think we've all been through enough," I chime in. "I vote for keeping ourselves safe. It's been hard enough on us women, but some of you," I glance at Zar, "have been slaves your whole lives. I vote we do what we must to ensure we get to lead decent, safe lives. If that means…" I sputter to a stop. I can't say the word kill, but hell, none of the males currently inhabiting the cell block risked their lives to help any of us.

Both males nod silently. I made my point.

"We've been throwing around ideas of where we're going to head after Numa. If you have any suggestions, let me know," Axxios says, changing the subject.

Zar shakes his head. "I only know planets with gladiator arenas. It would be nice to touch down somewhere that doesn't approve of slaves or fighting to the death. I hear there are planets like that."

"Some of the males have talked of Gaia. It's a mythical planet where peace has supposedly reigned for millennia. It's just slave talk, though. No place like that exists."

"We can't afford to chase dreams," Zar insists. "Getting ourselves to immediate safety has to be our first priority. We must protect the females."

"Yes, but we'll need some credits stashed away to accomplish that. Most of the males on board have no way to earn credits other than their skill in the arena."

Zar nods. "That's the only thing I've ever done, but not you, Axxios. You can go anywhere. Perhaps you can help us hire another captain. It's obvious you have another life you can return to. A better one."

"I've never shared my story with anyone on this ship, but you're stuck with me for the duration. I have nowhere else to go. None of us do. We're all in this together."

Axxios stands, thumps his chest with his fist and nods to Zar, then takes his leave.

"He's a good male," I observe.

"Aye."

Zar

I never really believed, not deep down in my heart, that I would ever be a free male. This amazes me more than having survived an almost-fatal stab wound with what Anya called a screwdriver, to the abdomen. But it does not amaze me more than that Anya is here by my side and telling me she loves me... over and over.

I'd assumed they would separate us on Hyperion and sell us off to different sectors of the galaxy. When I allowed myself to believe, even for a *minima*, that we'd take over this ship, I never thought Anya would want to stay with me when she had a choice. She's so delicate and smart and funny. And so beautiful. Why would she want to be with me? She told me I remind her of an apex predator on her homeworld. Why would she want that?

And yet, it seems she does. The look in her eyes when she gazes at me. The way she takes care of my needs as I lay in this bed, too sick to fend for myself, that speaks volumes.

Dr. Drayke told us there's not a lot more he can do for me. He says I'm on the mend and cleared me to leave medbay. Anya is cleaning the first mate's old room right now. For us! She's organizing a cabin we can share. My stomach does a flip, and not because of my injuries. It's still hard to believe we can stay together as long as we want.

"You ready?" Anya interrupts my thoughts. "Ready to go to our room? A room with a bed large enough for two? A room with a *door*?" She winks at me and waggles her eyebrows.

"I'm ready, Anya, but I don't think I'm in shape yet for..."

"I understand, babe. We've got all the time in the world for that."

She gives me a warm smile, reassuring me we have so many opportunities in front of us—together.

Anya

I brought Zar a size huge blue jumpsuit from the laundry. I'm acquainted closely enough with his anatomy that the hole I cut for his tail was in the perfect spot. It's so not fair that I look completely hideous in my blue jumpsuit, and he looks good enough to attack. Oh well, I think he'd look sexy in a tablecloth and lampshade.

He insists on walking to our new quarters even though I try to talk him out of it. I know he has a limited supply of energy, and I worry he'll have a relapse.

Most of the others "just happen" to be in the hallway as we slowly make our way to our new home. They're all so happy to see him. It's as if they're paying their respects. All the males do that chest thump/nod thing. The women all thank him out loud.

They divert us from going to the first mate's cabin and steer us to the captain's room.

"What's going on?" I ask.

"The females taught us what a vote was and insisted we take one," Shadow explains. "It was a unanimous decision. Zar, we elected you captain."

Everyone applauds. Hell, even Shadow seems to be smiling, if you could call his half-grimace a smile.

Zar cocks his head, his brows lowering as if this news doesn't thrill him.

"We'll take another vote when I'm well," his deep voice rumbles. "This crew deserves better than to be led by a trained gladiator who was almost killed by an untrained mech with a tool for screwing. I must have won with a sympathy vote."

A sudden laugh escapes my lips which is echoed by every woman in the hallway. Zar and all the males have the same confused look on their faces, only theirs show shock and anger that we would discuss Zar's near-death experience with laughter.

"It's an Earth phrase with another meaning. I'll explain later, big guy." I stroke his arm in reassurance, just as I see all the other women do the same with the males beside them.

Shadow shrugs. "We all bear the scars of the mistakes we have made. It was unanimous. Another vote won't change anything." His comment is more of a growl than spoken words. It appears the gentle, considerate Shadow I met in medbay has left the ship.

"Let's revisit this later," I say, as I give Zar's arm a pull. We head toward the cabin I'd prepared for the two of us while he'd been sleeping.

Finally, we're in our little room and for some unknown reason, I feel a bit shy. I show Zar around, though there's not much to see. The main room is maybe twice as big as our cell. Ah, but the bed, it's about the size of a queen bed back home. After what we've been sharing, it seems spacious.

There's a little closet, definitely big enough for two blue jumpsuits, a pair of moose PJs, and a scrap of loincloth. In the corner is the galaxy's smallest desk, which holds a computer and nothing more. I hope it has access to Google and Netflix, ha ha. Off the main area is a modest bathroom with another blessed door. I feel trendy. It's like a tiny house.

I help Zar pull off his jumpsuit, taking only the briefest moment to notice that despite the fact he's lost a few pounds during his convalescence, he's still so freaking sexy I can barely keep my hands off him. I help him into bed, wondering in the back of my mind if maybe he's well enough to make good use of a room with a closed door. Sadly, he falls soundly asleep as soon as his head hits the pillow. But the good news is we have pillows.

I climb in and spoon him from behind. On the tiny bed in our cell, he was always behind me. This is new and different. There are several inches between us, so I pull the covers

back enough to enjoy the visual of his muscular back and
tail.

I'd never really noticed, with everything bound up in that
loincloth, how sexy the little divot is at the top of his tail
where it connects to the meat of his ass. My fingers itch
to explore that little inch of masculine, feline territory. Not
today, I admonish myself. Poor baby needs his sleep.

His back and shoulders are so muscular, I can't keep my
hands off them. I softly rub the velvet fur that covers those
hard muscles from the top of the globes of his ass to the
harbor where shoulders meet neck. Then I sift my fingers
through his mane. He's totally out of it. I feel like a perv, but
it's so liberating to have free rein.

I must have dozed for a while. When my eyes pop open,
the computer's screensaver says it's time for dinner. I figure
we should join everyone in the little dining area. Zar needs
to eat, and I'm a little behind the curve in getting to know
everyone. The only opportunity I had to talk to any of the
others was when we were cleaning up after the Marauder
attack.

I shower his neck with tiny close-lipped kisses, softly scrape
the meat of his feline ears with my teeth, then hotly blow in
his ear. That seems to do the trick!

"Mmmm, who's doing that?"

My heart stutters for half a moment, wondering who he
thinks is attacking him if not me. Then he turns over, a sly
smile on his face, and I realize he's joking with me. He's
always been so serious. It's a revelation to discover Zar has
this soft, playful side.

He looks at me so tenderly, I decide maybe dinner was a bad
idea. Maybe we should just stay here and take advantage of
having a door. But he's weak, and has lost weight, and I really
need to get the poor guy nourishment.

"Let's get you up, Zar. I need to get some food in you."

His gaze locks on the door, "I've never had my own room before." He seems as excited about the privacy as I am.

"Well, big guy, you actually don't have your own room now. You have to share this with me. Unless you don't want to." I give him a deadpan stare.

He throws his heavy arm over me and pulls me closer. "It won't be that easy to leave my lair. Big, strong gladiators mostly get what they want, little Anya. And this gladiator wants you."

"Well then, you'll never get your own room, Zar. 'Cause I'm staying."

He holds my gaze for a long moment, then his eyes drift to my chest as his nostrils flare in arousal. Okay, I'm at a choice point. Attack handsome-but-weakened lion-man right now, or get him the nourishment he needs. I hop out of bed and slip into my sexy blue one-piece number while I hear his sensual groan.

He eases out of bed and pulls on his jumpsuit. I look back and forth between the two of us. Wasn't there a period in pop culture history where couples wore matching outfits? Was it the awful seventies? The terrible eighties? I know I saw some shockingly atrocious pictures on my Facebook throwback Thursday feed at some point. Luckily, I think that trend lasted about a minute, and for good reason! Not sexy then, definitely not sexy now. Oh well, it's all we've got.

"Come on, we're going to eat with the others. You need food."

"There are things I need more at the moment." He spears me with a molten gaze. He still hasn't completely shrugged into his suit.

"Look," I say, using a prim nurse Nancy kind of voice, "I'm in charge of your speedy recovery, sir, and I say food now, meet your other needs later." I pierce him with a firm look, then add, "On the double!" He gives me a confused look. I'm sure that didn't translate well, but he hits the auto-zip and is ready to go.

His nap seemed to replenish his energy, so we make it to the dining area in record time. It's kind of shocking how this area resembles every high school cafeteria I've ever seen. It's a long, narrow room with absolutely no decoration. Down the middle of the shallow space are several rectangular tables with benches on both sides. The only difference between the tables on our ship and the ones on Earth is that the benches here are tall enough to accommodate these massive males' height. One of the first things I notice when we enter the room is that all the women's legs are dangling and swinging like little kids sitting on adult furniture.

Everyone is laughing and joking and we're happily welcomed into the fold. Shadow seems almost insistent that we sit across from him. Okay, we *are* back in high school, and yet again, I don't think I'm at the popular kids' table. He was sitting alone on this side of the room.

Who knew that Maddie, the woman bunking with Stryker, was a real honest-to-goodness chef back on Earth? She's evidently been cooking all afternoon and brings us plates heaped with piles of unidentifiable food.

I pause a moment, apprehensive about digging in until all the women unanimously praise the food and encourage me not to be afraid.

"I had no idea what any of these things were," Maddie says. "It was like an episode of *Chopped* where I'm given a basket of unknown allegedly edible items and have to make something terrific out of it. I think I did pretty well."

The males all compliment the food, but hell, they've mostly been eating sawdust bars their whole lives. I look again at all the approving nods of the women and tuck in. "Yummmm." Frankly, I can't tell vegetables from meat or starch, but it's all pretty delicious.

While Zar and I are quickly working through the food on our plates, I notice he's having no trouble packing it in. Good. At this rate, he should regain his energy in no time.

"Sooo," I ask no one in particular, "if you don't mind me asking, what are the sleeping arrangements?" I've never been one to beat around the bush, and I'm dying to know how many of the couples have elected to stay together and which ones have separated.

"All of us women have chosen to bunk in our own rooms," Maddie informs me. "Most of us got along well with our male roommates," her eyes dart to Shadow, a disapproving scowl on her face, "but all of us, males *and* females, agreed it was too much, too soon. We wanted some time apart to figure out if there is real attraction or if it was just hormones and necessity." Her eyes widen and she immediately realizes she might have just insulted the crap out of Zar and me.

"Oh." She's backpedaling as quickly as possible, "I'm sure it's different with you and Zar." She's blushing. It's sweet.

I put my hand on Zar's blue-overalled thigh and glance up at him. He's looking apprehensive, probably wondering if I'm going to start questioning my own decisions. I leave him no time for worry and announce, "That sounds like sensible reasoning. But Zar and I are certain about our feelings."

I smile up at him and can see his facial muscles loosen in relief. Maddie looks calmer too. I'm sure she didn't want to start any problems.

Tyree slips in as if she's trying to snag some food and leave without being seen. I realize I haven't seen her since the overthrow. I've been so preoccupied with Zar's condition I haven't tried to contact her telepathically, nor have I heard from her. She realizes she can't just slink out, so she sits down across from me after grabbing a plate with almost no food on it.

Before I can give her a hard time about her absence, I inspect her face. Now it seems obvious why we haven't connected. She looks ill. Like death's door ill. I open my mouth to ask questions about her condition, but she launches before I can start talking.

She puts her hand up in a "stop" motion before I can give her any shit about her medical status. "I saw Dr. Drayke. He told me not to worry, I'm fine. I'm sorry I didn't visit while Zar was convalescing in medbay. Axxios has been teaching me how to function as first mate. He says I'm picking things up quickly. It's exciting. I think it's a great fit for my talents. I'm way more suited to it than joining the gladiators in the *ludus*."

I know she's trying to deflect my attention with her silly joke, but that doesn't diminish my worries about her health.

"I feel like a bad friend, but learning how to relieve Axxios at the helm seemed urgent." She moves the food around on her plate but doesn't bring fork to mouth.

Her skin seems taut across her bones, her eyes have no luster, and she's squinting like I do when I'm coming down with a migraine. "When was the last time you talked to the doc?" I don't buy her line that all is well with her.

"To be honest, it was before we took over the ship. I'll go see him right now." She gets up and scurries out. It's only after she's out the door that I realize she didn't have a bite to eat. I decide to pursue this tomorrow.

I look around and notice I like this sterile little dining room. When I imagine putting decorations on the wall, I realize I've gotten used to the thought that my old life will never be the same, that I will never return to Earth.

I can visualize birthdays and holidays shared over mystery meat meals here. Everyone seems calm and happy and optimistic about the future, even though we have no idea what it holds. That is, everyone's happy except for Shadow, who is glowering, sitting alone on the opposite bench of our table.

He averts his eyes as I inventory him. He looks humanoid—no one would give him a second glance if he arrived on Earth tomorrow—except for his prosthetics. One eye glows red and looks completely robotic. It's obvious no one made any effort to make his eye look human or blend with his face. In fact, just the opposite, his eye looks decidedly like clumsy first-gen Earth attempts at making metal robots.

And the scars, not just near his eye, but they crisscross his "good" arm, and cover much of his exposed flesh. All the males show evidence of their time as fighting machines, but his scars seem so much more obvious.

He glances across at Zar, and his entire facial expression changes. He lowers his brow and glowers for a moment, then motions with his head for me to look at the male next to me.

Zar, who seemed hale and hearty when we entered the dining hall just a few minutes ago, now seems pale, his muscles slack. He has no stamina at all.

"Can someone call Dr. Drayke?" I try to hide the rising panic in my voice.

Just a few moments later, the doc hustles in and uses his med-pad to take Zar's vitals.

"He's tired, but don't worry," he reassures. "If a few males could help him back to his quarters with as little effort on his part as possible, I'm sure he'll be better in the morning." He gives me a serious look and orders, "You call me first thing in the morning if he's still weak or tired. In fact, I'll be at your room at ten hundred to check on him."

Shadow is out of his seat before the doctor finishes his instructions and is about to lift Zar into his arms like a groom carrying his bride. As tired as Zar is, he's having none of it, but he does let Shadow help him back to our room. The farther they walk, the more heavily Zar leans on his newfound friend's shoulder.

Chapter Eighteen

ZAR

I must have completely passed out last night after Shadow helped me to our room. "Our room." I like the sound of that. I'm part of a pair. I have someone to protect, and someone to have my back.

Anya's warm, soft body is in my embrace as I spoon her from behind. She's changed since she became a free woman. Other than her concern over me, she seems calmer, less anxious. I could get used to this—lying in bed with my female, being lazy, sleeping late. But my cock tells me the time for sleeping is over. My body feels well-rested and ready to go.

I scoot closer, my aroused cock pressing against the curve of her ass. It seems to have a mind of its own, and my hips begin their own rhythm even as my hand reaches around to play with Anya's breasts.

I lick the center of my palm and use the moist friction on her nipple. I'm not sure if she's even awake, but her body responds, her hips grinding back against me. My fingers pluck at her hardened pink buds, first one and then the other. Anya makes a tiny moan in the back of her throat and presses her ass against me. My balls tighten at her sexual sound.

"Zar," she says lazily, still not fully awake.

I just keep plucking her tight nipples, then rolling them between my fingers. "Ohhh." An aroused moan escapes her lips. I keep fondling, trying to keep control over my desire to turn her over and mount her like a rutting beast.

"Glad you're feeling better. What a nice way to wake me up," her voice is sleepy as she presses her backside against me and lifts one leg up, her knee bent, her foot resting on my thigh. This allows my cock to ride the slit between her legs from behind.

"Computer," she commands, "contact the doctor and cancel our appointment."

"Yes," the robotic female voice responds.

"We have all the time in the world... and a door, Zar. What are you going to do to me?" Her voice is low, breathy. My cock bobs in response.

I'm not a talker. I'd prefer to show her. I lean my head around her and gently scrape the sharp tip of one fang across her nipple. She sucks in a quick, harsh intake of breath, then falls heavily on her back, giving me full access to all of her.

"Am I wet?" Her voice is deep and sexy. "Am I wet enough for you?"

"Let me check." I slip a finger between her legs and slide into her warm channel. "You're drenched, little Anya. Maybe I should inspect closer."

Crouching on my knees between her legs, I slowly lick up her thighs from her knees. I learned this move from her. I can tease, too.

"Oh, your tongue... will I ever get used to... ahh, so good." Her head falls heavily onto her pillow.

My tail circles her thigh, pulling her legs farther apart as I lick and nip, first one leg and then the other. When I near the juncture of her thighs, she squirms, jacking her bottom off the bed. So insistent. Two can play her teasing game. I make my way back down toward her knee again.

"Not fair, Zar. Come up."

She grabs under my arms to pull me up toward the vee between her legs.

"I outweigh you by twice, little Anya. I'll get there when I'm ready." Then I move up her sensitive inner thigh, nipping on that responsive spot on the tender area right beside her patch of hair.

"Please..."

"When I'm good and ready." I blow on her sensitive nub. She practically levitates off the bed.

After a few more moments, I take pity on her and lick her with the raspy flat of my tongue.

"God," is all she can say through a long, low moan.

In a swift flurry, I flick the tiny tip of her clit. She tosses her head back and forth against the pillow. Then I press my tongue against the little dip at the side of her responsive button. I've discovered it's her favorite spot. She's completely lost now, just moaning and thrashing her head. Her hands tangle in the sheets. Her pink lips are moist and open—up above and down below.

I know I could push her over the edge right now with just the slightest penetration, but I love prolonging her pleasure. I move away from that spot for a moment. There might be such a thing as too much if I stay there. As soon as her body relaxes the slightest bit, I nip at the juncture of her thigh and torso for a moment. Then I return to her favorite spot. If anything, she's ramped up even higher.

She's in such a haze of pleasure I don't know how she finds the presence of mind to say, "Don't make me beg, Zar." In the next moment, she begs in a breathy voice. "Please."

I move on top of her, my weight on my forearms, as I wait for her to open her eyes so I can stare into her soul. My cock slides up and down her slit until we're both drenched in her juices, then I spear into her, filling her up until I'm fully seated.

The act of filling her, merging with her, transcends our physical coupling. It joins our souls. Just when I think I couldn't love her more, my chest explodes with warmth and tenderness.

Her arms curl around me, pressing my furred body against her slick skin. I match my rhythm to the dance of her hips. She moans, and I know she's almost there. I press harder, swiveling at the end of every thrust. Her inner muscles clamp down on my cock and quiver in what seems like an endless orgasm. With each wave of contractions, her keening moan intensifies. Finally, she screams my name in an ultimate spasm of ecstasy.

Acting completely on impulse, I flip her over and hoist her around her waist, lifting her onto all-fours. Seeing her from behind like this brings out the animal in me.

This is nothing like our forced matings in the cell when I took her from behind to spare her feelings. I've discarded my higher mind and am functioning on primitive impulse.

My cock kicks impatiently and I spear into her in one determined surge. My claws extend. My gums itch. An unknown need spirals up from my belly, making my mouth water.

I passed desire long ago. Lust is far behind me. I'm in urgent territory. Desperate. Feral.

Opening my mouth wider than it's ever been, I latch my teeth around her shoulder and press. I'm not breaking the skin, but the tips of my four canines are on the cusp of stabbing into her.

Her head whips to the side. Our gazes meet over her shoulder. Her eyes are wide, terrified, then she takes a deep breath.

"You want to do this?" she asks, somehow knowing my intent.

I nod my head almost imperceptibly, my mouth still latched to her flesh.

"Go for it, big guy. I trust you."

I thought she'd look away to better tolerate the pain, but she keeps us tethered through our gaze.

My hips had paused, but with Anya onboard, they regain their rhythm. The look on my mate's beautiful face tells me she doesn't know whether to delve into her arousal or fly away in terror.

Her hips decide for her as they drive backward, urging me on, spiraling us both higher.

At the moment of her release, when her lids close in bliss, I pound into her, carrying us both away. When I come, my jaws close on her tender flesh as I growl deep in my throat.

She mewls in pain for the swiftest moment, but before guilt can overtake me, her channel spasms around mine with such ferocity I wonder how she can live through the torrential storm of her release.

Her head hits the mattress as she arches her back and thrusts her ass toward me like an offering to a god. My teeth are still embedded in her flesh, so I'm jackknifed over her as her spasms slow and finally stop. She whimpers, dazed, spent, and boneless.

I release her and lick her wounds, not sure whether to hide my face in guilt or shout in triumph. I do neither. Completely without warning, an ear-splitting roar escapes my mouth. Then another. And another. My head jerks back in surprise. I don't even know how my body created that sound.

"Whoa, what was that?" she asks, still descending from her intense peak of pleasure.

"I'd completely forgotten. Something Pallatin told me so long ago it feels like another lifetime. He told me when you find your life's truemate you begin to roar. I'd only half-believed it, and knew I'd never find my life's mate anyway, so it was archived in the farthest reaches of my brain."

"Truemate, huh?"

"He said the Ton'arr mate for life. When you find your truemate you never separate, you never want another, you love them with all your heart until you cease to exist."

Anya

I'm not exactly sure what to say. It sounds kind of like marriage, only the forever kind, not the sixty-percent-get-divorced kind.

I realize we've only known each other a short time, but I think I've learned everything I need to know about Zar. When you weather a storm together, or in our case, go through a revolution together, you get a pretty damn good grasp of someone's character.

Guys I'd been with in the past could barely be counted on to show up on time for a date, much less be willing to die in a laser fight for me. Yeah, I guess it doesn't sound like a hardship to be a truemate for life to the world's sexiest lion-man.

"Well, if you were asking if I'm okay with that, the answer's definitely yes."

"How's your shoulder?"

"Will I bear the mark?" she asks, her eyes bright with excitement. "I'd like that. As soon as you licked me, the pain disappeared."

"Good. I'd never want to hurt you, Beloved."

He smiles happily. I do love it when he hits me with one of his rare smiles. I have a feeling I'll be seeing a lot more of them in the future. Shortly after his full weight hits the bed and he nestles in behind me, he dozes off, his arm around my waist. We both love to spoon, even on this bigger bed.

I'm lazily rubbing the fur on Zar's hip and thigh, enjoying the afterglow of our lovemaking. Finally, I got to scream in pleasure with the knowledge we were blessedly alone.

He got to scream, too—in his own way. Truemate. I did not see that coming. But it doesn't scare me. Hell, I've been through so much lately I don't think lasting happiness should scare me at all. Not only have I found Zar, but I've found myself.

The woman I was a few short weeks ago was bored and listless and her life was going nowhere. Now I've spearheaded a freaking revolution, for God's sake.

I don't know where I'll be in the future. Like, literally don't know where in the galaxy I'll be. But I know I'll be going somewhere. And I know I'll be with Zar. And there's not much more I could ask for.

Epilogue

ANYA

"Count them again," Zar snarls.

"I can count them a hundred times more," Shadow snaps. "Unanimous is unanimous." With the way he's rolling his eyes, if he weren't a big, muscled gladiator, he'd be a junior high school girl.

"Unanimous sounds pretty decisive," I say as I thread my fingers through Zar's. "They've elected you captain. Accept with grace."

Somehow, his gaze loses its angry fire on the trip between staring down Shadow and gazing at me with love.

"Yes, my Anya. You're right, as usual." After dipping his lips to the top of my head for the briefest, softest kiss, he raises his voice for everyone assembled in the dining room to hear. "Since you've all voted for me, even in the recount, I appreciate your faith in me and accept the position of captain."

Everyone on the ship is here, but none can see the way his fingers squeeze mine. Funny how he's been my lifeline through the insurrection, but I'm the person he counts on when he feels insecure.

"Your trust in me is serious, and I will hold this position with honor. It's a lot of responsibility to captain a ship while being chased by the MarZan cartel and possibly the Galactic

Federation as well. I promise to carry out my duties to the best of my ability to show you I'm worthy of your faith and trust."

He looks every one of them in the eyes and nods, expressing his sincerity. They all clap, the males pounding their chest and nodding, giving him their utmost respect.

"As my first order of business, I'm told that on Earth, ship captains are empowered to conduct what my Anya calls ménage ceremonies."

While he's smiling his proud and terrifying grin, with those deadly fangs exposed, I correct, "Marriage."

"Marriage," he says. "My lovely Anya said she wanted to be marriaged, and I'd like everyone in attendance to give us your blessing."

He's so adorable. Every day that passes, he loosens up a bit, just making him more loveable. I'm not sure if mangling those words is a joke, or just some glitch in our translators.

"When will the nuptials be?" Axxios, the golden pilot asks in that formal way he has of speaking.

"Right now," Zar says. "I've written it out."

Several emotions slice through me, twining and dancing along my veins. I love him with all my heart, so I don't know why I experience a frisson of fear. The second feeling is a tidal wave of love washing through me.

I'd mentioned a marriage ceremony, but I never expected it. Certainly not now. We're still wearing our matching blue jumpsuits. I've cut and sewn the hems, but they're as heinous as they were before, just less of a tripping hazard.

"Now?" I stage whisper to Zar.

"What better time? We arrive on planet Numa tomorrow." He dips his head closer and speaks softly enough only I can hear. "We plan to change our ident numbers, repair the damage from the Marauder attack, and buy clothes that fit you little Earth females. But our enemies could be waiting for us there. I want you to have this. I want *both* of us to have this. Does it matter what you wear? Shouldn't it be about what's in your heart?"

Putting it like that reminds me what the point of the ceremony is—commitment. Enormous blue jumpsuit or white gown, it shouldn't make a difference.

"Yes. It should be about what's in our hearts. Let's get married."

Here we are in the dining room of a ship we just took over in an armed insurrection. We're surrounded by our comrades. If we live long enough, I hope they become our friends. They're standing, gathered around us, every single face beaming with happiness, which, I'm sure, reflects back to them in the expressions on our faces.

I push all of that to the back of my mind. The fear of the future, the worries about such a big commitment, wondering what awaits us on Numa and beyond. It strikes me that even if I'd courted a man on Earth for years, I'd still have the same jitters on my wedding day. You never know what the future holds. You can only trust in the power of love.

Zar and I love each other enough to stand together no matter what the future holds.

He reaches into a pocket of his dark blue jumpsuit and brings out a folded slip of paper. I don't know where he found paper. Everything seems to be written on computers on this ship.

My lion-man ran into the engine room, facing death, without a moment's hesitation. Now, though, his hands are trembling with the weight of what we're about to do. For some reason, this soothes me. To know he's not taking this lightly, that this ceremony is as meaningful to him as it is to me, is reassuring.

"Welcome to our mating ceremony," Zar intones, his gaze flicking to the assembly. "Thank you for giving your blessing to my union with my beloved Anya."

His golden eyes find mine, and the muscles on his face soften. Everything in the room fades away, and it's just Zar and me. All the butterflies that had swarmed in my chest evaporate. How could I hold onto any emotion but love right now? With him gazing at me with so much affection, there's no room in my chest for anything but warm swells of love.

"I was a slab of living granite the day I met you. The muscle inside my chest beat, but I was a walking automaton. I'd become so accustomed to death, I forgot what life was."

His head dips imperceptibly toward me, as if he wanted to punctuate his words with a kiss, but he draws back to his full height to continue.

"All of that changed the day I met you. You thawed my heart, chiseled away the layers I'd wrapped around it, and found the person inside me who had been lost for a long time."

My chest tightens and I swallow a couple times, fighting back my happy tears. He's already grown so much, come so far from the male I met in that cell only a few days ago. I wonder what other changes are in store as we grow old together.

"You are my truemate. The other half of my heart and soul. I promise you honesty, faithfulness, affection, and protection, Anya. But most of all, I promise you love."

My knees dip as the sweetest emotion sweeps over me with the force of a tsunami.

It hits me that I should respond. He'd prepared, brought some notes. I can only speak from my heart.

"I didn't believe in soulmates, or truemates as you call them. I do now. I promise to be your confidant, your friend, and your trusted advisor. Most of all, I promise to love you with all my heart. Forever."

My words may not have been practiced, but they brought a wide, fanged smile to Zar's face. I think it will be a few more weeks before those long canines no longer trigger the immediate desire to run from an apex predator.

"Kiss the bride!" Savannah calls.

When Zar doesn't immediately comply, a chorus of feminine voices chants, "Kiss the bride. Kiss the bride." On the next round, all the males chime in.

"Here?" Zar asks.

"Give it your best, babe."

Instead of bending to my level, he grips me around my waist and lifts me to his. Before he kisses me, he places his lips to my ear.

"This is what you wanted, my beloved? Was this the mating ceremony of your dreams?"

"Far from it, big guy. This was so much better."

"Aye." His lips descend to mine and everything else fades away.

Two weeks ago, if someone told me aliens were real and being abducted would be the best thing to ever happen to me, I would have laughed myself sick. I can't believe how my life has changed in so short a time. I don't know what the future holds, but I know I'll face it with a helpmate, a soulmate, my lover and best friend who I'm now married to. My beloved. My Zar.

Dear Reader

I HOPE YOU ENJOYED <u>Zar,</u> the first in the Galaxy Gladiator Series Keep reading to get a peek at Shadow's story, which is the next in the series. But wait! I've written a novelette with Shadow's backstory to help explain why he's such an angsty jerk. Sign up to my newsletter to read his backstory. I know he's a dick, but I promise, he's fully redeemed by the end of his book. My newsletter will be full of early peeks, cover releases, extra content, giveaways, and other fun stuff.

There are twenty other Galaxy Gladiator books just waiting to be read. Zar and Anya even have a very exciting sequel (but that's #18) So, what are you waiting for? This might be the time to catch up with all the alien male lusciousness waiting for you.

Scroll for Shadow's first chapter. Keep scrolling for a list of all my series.

Free Newsletter Signup

Request for Reviews: Reviews equal love for an author, and also help us keep writing. Please take a moment to rate this book. If you write a review I promise I read every single one.

Hugs,

Alana

Sneak Peek: Shadow

PRESENT DAY

Planet Numa

Chapter One

Petra

I thought for a moment if I just shut my eyes and opened them again, this shitshow would disappear. I've tried three times now to no avail. It's official. I'm having a really bad day. Actually, I've had several in a row.

I was kidnapped from my bed by aliens who beamed me onto their spacecraft. The ugly, boar-like guys shoved me unceremoniously into a coffin-shaped pod, which filled with rotten-egg-smelling gas and knocked me out.

I have no idea how long I was lying unconscious, but I woke up about an hour ago. The boar people roughly inserted a translator under the skin behind my right ear. Then they marched me off the ship into this enormous, decrepit building, and threw me into the barred cell I'm currently occupying.

It's disorienting and terrifying to go from Earth to a spaceship capable of interstellar travel, to the dank dungeon I inhabit. It's like transporting from the future to the dark ages in the span of an hour.

The floor is a jigsaw puzzle of stone; the cells are crudely constructed of metal bars on three sides with a back wall of rock and mortar. The lighting flickers haphazardly; drops of cool water occasionally drip off the dank ceiling onto my hair and face.

Rubbing my clammy, shaking hands on my thighs, I straighten my shoulders. I have no time for self-pity, sadness, or fear. First things first. I need to focus and get my bearings. I have to figure out why I'm here, who's in charge, and how to get the heck back home to my life on Earth.

I don't see any guards, only the inhabitants of the two adjoining cells. I'm still not over the fact that aliens aren't just a feature on the SYFY network. There are women of two different alien species on either side of me, which blows my mind. The fact that I'm standing here is proof positive UFOs *are* real.

The humanoid woman, or should I say female, to my right looks vaguely reptilian with roughly textured greenish-brown skin and flat, elongated nostrils. She hasn't stopped crying since my arrival. At least I think she's crying; her high-pitched whine is piercing my eardrums. Paying attention to my irritation seems far better than tuning in to the terror coiling in the pit of my stomach.

I figure getting her to talk to me would kill three birds with one stone. I'd hopefully collect some info, keep my mind off the icy horror speeding through my veins, and perhaps she would stop making that horrific noise.

"Hi, I'm Petra." After waiting a moment for her to respond, I try again. "Hello, can you understand me?"

She looks at me, eyes narrowed in distrust, then finally responds, "I'm Zanek."

"I just arrived here. Where are we? Who's in charge? What do they want?" I'm desperate for answers.

"I... I," she sputters to a stop. She pulls herself together, squares her shoulders and takes a deep breath. "We're on planet Numa, I believe. It's where slavers go to buy and sell their wares. They have houses of pleasure, sex exhibitions, and gladiator fights." She points with a lift of her chin toward an open doorway.

I hadn't paid attention until now, but I can see through the narrow opening into a massive arena. Across the covered stadium are hundreds of crude benches in a stepped fashion rising toward the roof. Aliens of all types, shapes, and colors are excitedly filing toward their seats. I can hear the low buzz of animated discussion.

"That's a stadium for fighting right there?"

She nods.

"Are they going to fight us against each other?" I can't control the shrill tone of my voice as a spike of fear races up my spine.

"I doubt it. I assumed they were holding us here for a slave auction, perhaps tomorrow."

Slaves? Hell no! That's what they dragged me across the universe for? I want to believe this is just a dream, that there aren't such things as aliens and spaceships. But looking at this dungeon and the reptilian woman less than ten feet away—it's obviously true.

Cold tentacles of fear grab at the edges of my thoughts, but I push them away. That I've been kidnapped and hauled to another part of the galaxy to be sold as a slave has to be relegated to the back attic of my mind—like so many other things I've endured in my life. My goal right now is to figure out how to escape.

"Slaves? This can't be true," I insist, even though the facts support it.

She can't meet my gaze and resumes her shrill wailing. She manages to spit out "sex slaves," then completely loses it.

She's weeping so hard I know she's incapable of answering any more questions, at least for the moment.

I've noticed the female in the cell to my left has been listening to our conversation. She has a noisy bubbler device attached to her nose and mouth; I assume she can't breathe the air on this planet without it.

"Is this true?" I ask, still in denial.

She nods, then points to the breathing apparatus on her face. She obviously won't be able to answer any more questions.

I pace for a moment, trying to get a grasp on the situation. Okay, sex slave on a planet so far from home I had to be put in suspended animation to get here. It's clear. No one is coming to save me.

I'm not going to lose my focus. I *will* get myself out of this. I've coped with bad situations before. I'm twenty-eight years old. I can think rationally. I have resources, albeit not many. At least I'm not four years old and living in war-torn Serbia anymore. Thoughts of my experiences as a little girl in a war zone, threaten to intrude. I forcefully push them away. I am *not* a vulnerable, fearful little girl; I'm going to figure a way out of this.

It's hard to see beyond the arched doorway into the stadium. What strikes me more than the dirt floor, risers and seats is the energized air of excited expectancy. How can these people be capable of space travel, yet still so barbaric as to enjoy gladiatorial flights?

"Petra, concentrate!" I scold myself; I need to plot a way out of here. I've got to get home to my friends. My eyebrows pull together in worry about my cat, Mooshie. I hope my roommate keeps him fed until I get home.

My attention darts to three people striding down the corridor outside my cell toward the arena. One guy is enormous, like a seven-foot Norse god—snow-white hair, piercing blue eyes, and built like a linebacker, only bigger.

The other male is something out of a dystopian nightmare. He's also big and muscular, but his resemblance to his friend stops there. He's humanoid with a kind of Borg-like prosthetic left eye that shines red and a mechanical left arm. He's wearing only a loincloth.

I can't tear my eyes away, but I'm not sure whether it's from repulsion or fascination. His body is jaw-droppingly well-muscled, but it's also heavily scarred from face to knees. He has an angsty rage I can smell from one hundred yards away. Even a million miles from Earth, I can't get away from that magnetic attraction to the bad boys? There is definitely something wrong with me.

Almost as an afterthought, I notice there's a female with them. I glance again to make certain, but I think she's human.

They are a few doors down from my cell when I call out, "Are you from Earth? Can you help me?"

Her head snaps over in my direction; she looks me up and down as her eyes narrow. She seems skeptical.

"You're human? Where are you from?" She asks warily.

"Serbia originally, Philly most of my life."

Still suspicious, she asks, "What's your football team?" Like knowing this would prove I'm really from Earth.

"The Eagles. I just woke up here. Can you help me?"

She and the Norse god are both wearing blue jumpsuits. She looks up at him. He leans his head down to her and they confer. The discussion appears to be progressing into a whisper-fight. I think she's pleading my case. He doesn't seem convinced. The bad boy seems utterly disinterested in them or me and is peering impatiently through the archway into the arena.

"Please!" I try to keep her focused on coming to my aid. "I've been kidnapped from Earth and brought here. The female in the next cell told me they're going to sell me as a sex slave. I've done nothing wrong. Can you help me?"

She seems to redouble her efforts to convince the big guy to help. They've moved closer to my cell and I catch snippets of their conversation.

"We can't leave her here, Theos. She's human, like me. We fought our owners and won our own freedom less than a week ago. I can't walk away from another of my kind and abandon her to be sold as a slave."

"Why her? Why not the beings on either side of her? Why not everyone on this entire cell block? We can't save everyone, Savannah."

"You're right. We can't save everyone. But maybe we can save *her*. She's human like me and all the other females on the ship. You wouldn't leave a fallen comrade, would you? It's like that—I can't walk away!"

He's so much bigger than her, but he doesn't pull rank or order her around. He seems to be listening to her and considering things from every angle.

"We have no money, Savannah. That's why we're here on this shit planet to begin with. That's why Shadow is getting ready to fight in this arena. We need credits to repair our ship, for food and necessities. We already have over twenty souls to take care of. We're not even sure we can manage that, much less add one more mouth to feed. We can't break this female out; this facility is too heavily guarded. The only way to rescue her is to buy her. Where will we find the money for that?"

"I'll earn it," I interrupt eagerly.

They quit arguing and their heads swivel to look at me, skepticism written all over their faces.

"Get me out of here and I can earn money." My mind is racing, but I've always been a hard worker. I'll do anything to get out of this cell.

"How?"

"I cut hair. I'm sure there's a need for a good hairdresser…"

A deep scratchy voice intrudes over a loudspeaker in the arena. A roar goes up from the crowd. Sexy loincloth guy cracks his knuckles and his neck, then announces arrogantly, "I have to find the promoter. I told you both from the beginning, I don't need you here. I certainly don't need to help with this pathetic little human's problems. I'll find you after I win my match." He turns on his heel, not waiting for a reply.

"We'll be right here," Savannah forcefully points to the floor where she's standing, an obvious statement she's not leaving. Theos merely nods.

"Look," Savannah resumes our conversation, talking confidentially, her eyes suspiciously scanning the other prisoners. "Me and nine other Earth women were kidnapped less than a month ago and placed on a slave ship with ten gladiators, also slaves. A week or so ago, we overthrew our guards and we're now in possession of the vessel and our freedom. We came directly to this planet to make necessary repairs, get some forged credentials, and make enough credits to pay for it all.

"We'll be leaving as soon as the repairs are completed—we've got some bad guys on our tail. We can't dawdle around this hell hole so you can cut hair. Money is tight. I don't know where we'd get enough to buy you."

"She," I point my thumb at the reptilian girl, "tells me there are a lot of sex clubs on this planet. Are there strip clubs?"

Savannah's eyes widen. "Are you offering to sell your body to avoid slavery?"

"I have… skills. I'll do whatever it takes to get myself out of this cell and leave this planet on your ship as a free woman. You buy me and take me to a strip club. Lend me one of your gladiators to protect me while I work, and I won't stop until I've paid you back."

Theos has been listening intently and now shakes his handsome head back and forth. "No, this won't work. We don't even know how much it will cost to buy her. She has no idea how much she can make doing... whatever it is she will do. It's a terrible plan. It isn't even a plan, Savannah, it's just a wish. I vote no."

Savannah looks trapped. I'm afraid she agrees with him.

"Look. How about if I promise a money-back guarantee? He's right. I have no idea how much I'll cost or how much I can make. But if I haven't earned enough to pay you back by the time the repairs are complete and you're ready to fly, you can sell me back to the people you buy me from. No loss to you." I don't know what I'll do if I have to return to this cell, but at least this gives me a fighting chance.

"Theos, look, she's giving us a guarantee," Savannah coaxes. "This is a no-lose situation... except for her. She's willing to fight for her freedom. Which is exactly what we just did on the ship. Please, let her try."

He inhales deeply and thinks for so long I assume I've lost the battle. Then he takes another breath and nods almost imperceptibly. "I'll comm the ship and run it by the captain. If he agrees, I'll help."

A few minutes later, he informs us, "Captain Zar agreed, but he insists on holding her to the guarantee. We can't afford to put everyone's life at risk for this, as much as we all want to help."

The needs of the many outweigh the needs of the few, one of my favorite quotes from *Star Trek* is being thrown back in my face, darn it.

Theos stalks off in search of someone in a position of authority who can negotiate a price for me. I don't bother with false modesty as I yank off my knee-high black boots, pull my panties off, stash them in my bra, and drag my leggings back on.

While we wait for Theos, my eyes stray into the arena when I hear the crowd roar with appreciation. I'm just in time to see a monstrous, green reptilian with several rows of teeth in his enormous mouth smash his smaller, humanoid opponent so hard the man drops to the dirt, unable to get up. At first, I think he's dead, but after a moment, I can see his chest weakly rising and falling.

The announcer then calls two names for the next match. "That's Shadow's fight," Savannah informs me with as much concern as if she's ordering Starbucks.

"Aren't you distressed? Worried he'll be hurt? The guy who lost the previous fight looks like he might never recover."

"Shadow's a dick," she lifts her shoulders. "I guess it would be a shame if he got severely injured, but..." She shrugs again and tilts her head.

This stuns me. I'm trusting these people to keep me safe, and this woman doesn't seem to care if her comrade lives or dies. "Must be a really big dick," I muse out loud.

"We don't know each other well," she backtracks. "We were isolated as couples in cells until recently so I haven't spent much time with him. He just... didn't make a very good impression on many of us. He's angry. He's not sociable. But he did battle for our freedom. And," she adds almost as an afterthought, "he saved our captain's life."

"Okay, so we should both root for him in this fight, right?"

She lifts one shoulder noncommittally.

A commotion from the crowd draws my attention to the arena. I can only see a sliver of the action as I crane my neck to look through the slim, stone doorway. Shadow is matched against a tall Neanderthal-looking alien who must outweigh him by over fifty pounds. I look twice, thinking my eyes are playing tricks on me, but they're not. These guys are fighting in the nude.

I have to give him credit; Shadow's body is total eye candy. Did Savannah know how right she was when she called him a "dick"? Because every single female watching this match has to have that word pounding insistently through her mind right now. I have to pull my thoughts out of the gutter to give my attention to the actual fight.

In the hallway, I was struck by what a large man Shadow is, but now that he's out in the arena with that huge caveman, he's dwarfed. I don't know whether the bionic arm will be an asset or not, but he'll need some help if he's going to win. And he'd better win because I'm assuming it's the purse from this fight that's going to bankroll my get-out-of-jail-not-so-free plan.

Just as the Neanderthal is fiercely pounding Shadow in the chest, Theos and a shaggy blue alien approach my cell.

"I'm telling you," the blue guy says, his features slack from boredom, "I can't accept less than 50,000 credits."

"That's crazy," Theos insists, "I doubt our fighter will make much more than that in his fight against that gargantuan monster out there."

"Exactly. Whoever buys this lovely specimen of femininity will get her for her entire lifespan, as well as any progeny she may produce. Obviously, she should bring a higher price than a moment's prowess in the arena."

"I'm not authorized to pay that much. No more than 25,000."

"45,000 is as low as I can go."

"27,500," Theos offers, and I can tell he's struggling with the enormity of that sum.

"45,000 firm. I won't accept a credit less."

Shit. Not only do we have to get him down to a ballpark the gladiator can afford, but I have to get the price down to an amount I can pay back!

"Mmmmm," I say and begin to twitch. "Mmmmmmmm." My right leg starts shaking. "Ack. Ack. Ack." I act as if I'm about to dislodge a hairball.

"Ack." Twitch. "Ack." Twitch.

I begin to pull at my hair and moan.

"42,500," blue guy offers, looking at me like I'm a turd in the punchbowl.

My moan begins to ramp into a soft scream. I flop onto my knees and begin to move my right leg in imitation of a dog who loves where you're scratching it.

"Mmmmmm," I'm amplifying to a louder scream.

"40,000 is as low as I can go." Blue guy's staring down his nose at me in disgust.

I stand up and whirl around as I tip my head forward and back, my long hair flipping wildly. I'm making guttural noises in the back of my throat. Abruptly, I stop and stare directly at him and shriek. I could be wrong, but I think there's a hush in the arena for a moment in response to my prolonged wail.

"35,000 is as low as I can go, and only because I like you," the slaver's tone is oily and insincere.

I catch a glance between Theos and Savannah, and I believe they're both wondering if this is an act, or if I'm actually as crazy as I look.

I stand on the bed and begin to jump on it, now squawking like a bird. I'm not stopping until the price comes down some more.

"30," blue guy offers. It looks to me like he's getting nervous.

Theos shakes his head no.

"25?" Sounds like he's almost pleading now.

"No, she's clearly crazy. I don't think we want her at all."

I'm jumping and moaning now. Something big is happening in the arena. There's a lot of cheering. I hope Shadow is winning. I don't think they'll buy me if they don't get the prize money.

"15. You were right, my friend. I was inflating the price a moment ago. Greed is a terrible character flaw. I think you're right, 50 is far too high. 15 is fair."

Still jumping, my noises morph into those of a gorilla. I put my hands in my armpits like an ape. I stick my hands in my face as if to catch the smell of my underarms. Sniffing deeply, I release a satisfied moan.

"10. I can let her go for 10,000," his tone is urgent. I catch a quick glimpse of his expression. His nostrils are flared, head tipped back in pure disgust.

I glimpse Shadow stalking through the arched doorway. He's been beaten up—his pec is beginning to bruise and blood is dripping from an eye that's already half-closed. He's holding something aloft that must be credits, because he looks pretty proud of himself.

"Well..." I hear Theos hedge. I think he's about to agree to the ten thousand credits, but I'm still not certain I can pay that much back. I decide to go for the gold and get the price as low as possible.

I jump off the bed and spear the blue guy right in the eye with my gaze. I squat and while staring directly at him I release an orgasmic moan from deep in the back of my throat, and pee right in my pants. It's comical to see the look on their faces. I watch as blue guy, Theos, Savannah, and Shadow initially aren't sure what's happening. I'm wearing black leggings, so it's hard to see the wet spot. Then they see the puddle of urine pooling on the floor near my bare feet.

"5,000. I'll let her go for 5,000 if you pay it right this *modicum* and leave." He steps backward as if my puddle of pee was going to attack him.

Theos snatches the card from Shadow, hands it to the slaver who swipes it and opens the door to my cell as fast as possible.

I turn my back on all of them, pull off my sopping leggings, pull on my dry panties and my boots, and hurry after them down the corridor and out of the building.

Continue reading Shadow here.

Many Thanks

It TAKES A VILLAGE to write a book. I admit, I do all the heavy lifting, but my early reading teams help polish the gem.

Amarra Skye (my daughter and also an author) sat with me for hours in my basement office as we plotted a lot of my first three books. She continues to be my go-to when I'm lost.

Dr. Lee, my Developmental Editor and friend and Stephanie A., my Assistant and friend, read it first. Then it goes to my Alpha and then Beta Teams. Finally my Advance Reading Team gets it. There are numerous edits along the way.

Thanks to: Hilga H., Christine R., Sarah B., Marianne K., Gill V., Anushcka-Marie W., Kaye S.

Glossary

Annum—year

Cestus Gladiators—ancient form of gladiatorial combat like wrestling. Performed in the nude.

Drack—the perfect all-purpose expletive. It's a noun, it's a verb, it's an adjective.

Fierto—foot

Hoara—hour

Ince—inch

Ludus—gymnasium or training area for gladiators.

Lunar cycle—month

Mille—mile

Minima—minute

Modicum—second

Mullesta—fine fabric

Ton'arr—Zar's race of lion people

Trident—three-pronged spear.

About Alana Khan

Alana Khan is a Pinnacle Award-winning, USA TODAY Best-selling author whose pen traverses galaxies and explores the extraordinary.

In a life as diverse as her stories, Alana boasts IMDB film credits, thrilling Harley adventures on open roads, and a stint as a professional spoon player—because, why not?

With a background as a psychotherapist, she delves into the human psyche, enriching her storytelling.

Join her on fantastical journeys through her novels, where cosmic romance and monstrous love merge with spice as hot as a Carolina Reaper chili pepper.

Want to read the next books in the series? Check out Alana's other books? Help yourself to 15% off anything in the store including dozens of $5.99 audios.

Go to my website for FREE books at
http://www.alanakhan.com/

My Shopify Store

Website:

<u>Bookbub:</u>

<u>Goodreads:</u>

<u>Twitter:</u>

<u>Facebook:</u>

<u>Allmylinks:</u>

<u>Amazon Author Page:</u>

<u>Discover my channel on YouTube:</u>

Want more of my books?

Galaxy Gladiators Alien Abduction Romance Series

This 21-book series can be read as standalones, although it's fun to read them in order because the books are full of that rich, delicious found-family trope where people with nothing in common form connections that are stronger than blood. You'll grow to love this ragtag bunch of escaped slaves and the human women they rescue. Or do the women rescue them? Full of action, romance, and spice.

Galaxy Pirates Alien Abduction Romance Series

As the name implies, these alien Robin Hoods are scoundrels and rascals. Opportunists all, they've never met a human damsel in distress who wasn't worth saving. Full of action, romance, daring capers, and spice. P.S. The bad guys always lose their money and our pirates walk away all the richer.

Galaxy Sanctuary Alien Abduction Romance Series

There's one thing about flying across the galaxy righting wrongs (the Gladiator series) or stealing from people who deserve it (the Pirates series)--you can't have kids on a fighting ship. Some worthy freed gladiators end up on planet Fairea and find themselves on a safe parcel of acreage, yet in desperate need of funds. Between jostling for control of the operation and the lengths they must go to stay safe and keep the lights on, there is plenty of action, romance, and steam.

Galaxy Warriors Alien Abduction Romance Series

What was I thinking writing 19 books in the Galaxy Gladiators series? Call it temporary insanity. This series is similar to Gladiators, but lets new readers jump in without knowing any backstory. Action, adventure, my trademark spice, and romance.

Galaxy Games Hostile Planet Alien Romance Series

All the heart-pounding passion and gut-clenching action I could cram onto the page. This series will grab you by the throat from the first page and never let you go. More action and hotter than previous series. And love. Did I forget to mention love?

Awakened from the Ice Series

In a world where the past and present collide, the Awakened From the Ice series brings ancient Rome roaring into the 21st century. When a group of Roman gladiators, perfectly preserved in ice, are discovered and revived, the course of history is forever altered.

This series offers a unique blend of historical insight, futuristic technology, and timeless romance. With each awakening, new challenges arise, testing the bonds of friendship, loyalty, and love. Immerse yourself in this thrilling saga where ancient valor meets modern courage, and love proves to be the ultimate force of nature.

Rescued by the Monsters Reverse Harem Romance series

In a future dystopian Earth, males have been spliced with animal DNA. Human women have been reduced to chattel and when they say no, even once, they're banished Down Below to where the "monsters" live. This series will soon have you wondering just who the monsters are as the human women each bond with three adoring human/animal hybrids.

Wolven Warriors Series

In a world where fantasy meets the modern age, a pack of otherworldly protectors called the Wolven Warriors walks among us. These humanoid males, with their wolf-like features, dropped to Earth 25 years ago. Discover a captivating modern-day fantasy where romance ignites amidst danger, and the Wolven Warriors must fight not only for survival but for the forbidden love that binds them to their human soulmates.

Arixxia Fields: A Steamy Small-Town Alien Romance Series

Are you ready to party? I imagine so, after reading all the drama in all my previous series. Each of these books is short, sexy, romantic, and FUN. Each revolves around a holiday. Check them out.

Hybrid Hearts Series

Bred to be soldiers, these rescued genetically engineered males are all given a new lease on life. How does the United States military plan to do that? They create an isolated town with cute shops and train the males in new jobs. How about a sexy lion-man baker for starters?

Galaxy Artificials Series

Packed with passion and spice, USA TODAY Bestselling author Alana Khan brings robots to life in this science fiction romance series. Oh yeah, she manages to give the metallic buckets of bolts smokin' hot humanoid bodies, too.

Orcfire Series

Twenty-five years ago, thousands of Others (orcs, nagas, minotaurs, and other species only known in fairytales) fell onto the burning sands of the Mojave Desert with no way to go home. They were rounded up by the U.S. Military and placed in a fenced enclosure on the outskirts of Los Angeles. The OrcFire series features one hot, green, tusked orc as the hero of each book as they battle fires and so much more to find their happily ever after. The OrcFire series will be hot, hot, hot in all ways.

Treasured by the Zinn Alien Abduction Romance Series

The US government gave the Zinns permission to take human women as wives. Let's just say the unsuspecting women, who know nothing of this unsavory deal, are none too happy—until they fall in love.

Mastered by the Zinn Alien Abduction Romance Series

Welcome to the enticing universe of 'Mastered by the Zinn,' a secret arrangement that's endured for centuries. The government's shadowy pact with the alien Zinn species allows for the abduction of human women in exchange for cutting-edge military technology. It's a clandestine game of risk and reward, desire and dominance.